"Witch!" the voice hissed.

Alice Ramsay stirred, then raised her head, trying to focus her eyes. The small shed into which they had thrown her was windowless, the few fading rays of evening light from the opened door providing little illumination. A tall cloaked man stood silhouetted in the doorway. By the light of the candle in his hand, she was able to make out the man's features: the sharp black beard, trimmed to a point like a spearhead; the thick, heavy brows; and the features that might have almost been comely had they not been set in lines of cruelty and avarice. It was the face of a predator, of one who revelled in the pleasure of the hunt.

—from *The Witches of Willowmere*

Also by Alison Baird

PENGUIN CANADA

THE WITCHES OF WILLOWMERE

Alison Baird is the author of *The Wolves of Woden; The Hidden World; The Dragon's Egg,* which was nominated for the Ontario Library Associaton Silver Birch Award and designated a regional winner by the participating children; and *White as the Waves,* which was shortlisted for the IODE Violet Downey Book Award. Her next book will be *The Warding of Willowmere,* number two in the Willowmere series. She lives in Oakville, Ontario.

THE WITCHES OF
WILLOWMERE

ALISON BAIRD

PENGUIN CANADA

PENGUIN CANADA

Penguin Group (Canada), a division of Pearson Penguin Canada Inc.,
10 Alcorn Avenue, Toronto, Ontario M4V 3B2

Penguin Books Ltd, 80 Strand, London WC2R ORL, England
Penguin Putnam Inc., 375 Hudson Street, New York, New York 10014, U.S.A.
Penguin Books Australia Ltd, 250 Camberwell Road, Camberwell, Victoria 3124, Australia
Penguin Group (Ireland), 25 St. Stephen's Green, Dublin 2, Ireland
Penguin Books India (P) Ltd, 11, Community Centre, Panchsheel Park,
New Delhi – 110 017, India
Penguin Books (NZ) Ltd, cnr Rosedale and Airborne Roads, Albany, Auckland 1310,
New Zealand
Penguin Books (South Africa) (Pty) Ltd, 24 Sturdee Avenue, Rosebank 2196, South Africa

Penguin Books Ltd, Registered Offices: 80 Strand, London WC2R ORL, England

First published in Penguin Canada by Penguin Books, a division of Pearson Canada, 2002
Published in this edition, 2003

1 2 3 4 5 6 7 8 9 10 (TRS)

Copyright © Alison Baird, 2002

*Publisher's note: This book is a work of fiction. Names, characters, places and incidents
either are the product of the author's imagination or are used fictitiously, and any
resemblance to actual persons living or dead, events, or locales is entirely coincidental.*

Manufactured in Canada.

NATIONAL LIBRARY OF CANADA CATALOGUING IN PUBLICATION

Baird, Alison, 1963–
The witches of Willowmere / Alison Baird.

(Willowmere chronicles)
ISBN 0-14-301501-X

I. Title. II. Series: Baird, Alison, 1963– Willowmere chronicles.

PS8553.A367W58 2003   jC813'.54   C2003-901927-6
PZ7

Visit the Penguin Group (Canada) website at **www.penguin.ca**

For Judy Diehl
with many thanks

THE WITCHES OF
WILLOWMERE

PROLOGUE

Scotland, 1605 A.D.

"WITCH!" the voice hissed.

Alice Ramsay stirred, then raised her head, trying to focus her eyes. The small shed into which they had thrown her was windowless, the few fading rays of evening light from the opened door providing little illumination. A tall cloaked man stood silhouetted in the doorway. *It must,* she thought dazedly, *be one of the witch hunters—but which one?* Master Morley or Master King?

Then he moved closer, shutting the door behind him, and by the light of the candle in his hand, she was able to make out the man's features: the sharp black beard, trimmed to a point like a spearhead; the thick, heavy brows; and the features that might almost have been comely had they not been set in lines of cruelty and avarice. It was the face of a predator, of one who revelled in the pleasure of the hunt.

I

Master Morley. She wondered why he had come here. To question her yet again, or only to gloat over her?

"Rouse yourself, witch. Have you nothing to say before your trial?" demanded Morley, standing over her. "No word in your own defence?"

"What is the use?" the girl retorted without looking up at him. "I know well how these trials, as you are pleased to call them, proceed. One is assumed to be guilty of witchcraft from the moment the first accusation is made. No protestations of innocence will move any witch hunter. It is all a mockery of justice. But justice is not what you seek, is it?" She sat up and met his eyes with her own, her gaze steady and direct. He would not see that she was afraid. The fear and pain of others were meat and drink to this man. *Do not give him what he wants,* she thought.

He laid a hand on the front of his black velvet doublet. "I am a just man. I wish only to remove a taint of evil from—"

"You!" The words burst out of her. "You are no man! You are a fiend, and so is your accomplice. If the pair of you could not torment innocent folk, then any poor beast would do for you to hunt down and kill. Is that not so, Master Morley?" She looked away from him in disgust.

He set his candle down on a barrel and strode forward, seizing her hair and forcing her head around. "Where is he— your familiar spirit, the cat? Where has he gone? You will tell me! He will be wanted at the trial, to stand accused alongside you."

Alice thought of the white cat, all on his own now. He, at least, had escaped; the mob would not have him as well. "I do not know," she gasped. "How could I? I left my home two days ago. How can I know where my cat is?"

"Do not play the innocent, Mistress Ramsay! A witch always knows where her familiar is. Have you spoken with him since we brought you here?" She was silent, despite the tearing pain in her scalp. He released her hair and straightened, towering over her once more. "I can put you to torture, mistress."

"Then you will compel me to lie. That is all that torture achieves. The victims always recant afterwards, and so shall I."

He leaned closer, his dark eyes cold. There was nothing human in those eyes, she thought with a shudder. But they were not like an animal's either. What she saw in their lightless depths was pure malevolence, pure evil.

"It is one thing to lie to me. But will you lie to the court, mistress?" he asked softly. "When you are placed under oath, will you look the magistrate in the eye and say that you have no familiar? That the creature that accompanied you everywhere was a cat and nothing more? That you did not perform works of sorcery with his assistance? There were witnesses to many of your deeds, remember. How will you explain to the court the power that charms the creatures of forest and field, that can make a bird fly to your hand or stop a bolting horse in its tracks? Will you look them all in the eyes and lie?"

She could make no answer to that. Lie . . . she would have to, for who would believe the truth? But she would be a poor liar, she knew, and to utter false denial after false denial, under oath, before all those accusing eyes . . . Could she do it? Or would she break down in the end?

There was a glitter of triumph in Master Morley's eyes at her telltale hesitation. "Until later, Mistress Ramsay," he mocked, with a little bow.

Then the witch hunter took up his candle and strode out the door, slamming it shut and leaving Alice alone in the dark.

CHAPTER I

"SHE IS A *GODDESS!*" exclaimed a voice to Claire's right.

Claire, who was rummaging around for her biology text-book, glanced in the direction of the voice. The plump girl with pasty-looking skin who used the locker next to hers was standing in front of its open door with her friend, a small, thin Asian girl with thick-rimmed glasses. The two of them were staring fixedly at a magazine ad taped to the inside of the door. Claire pushed her own glasses higher up her nose and peered curiously over their shoulders at the picture. It showed an impossibly slender and elongated young woman reclining on an impossibly smooth and empty white beach. She was dressed—or rather, undressed—in a microscopic bikini that showed off her enormous bust and tiny waist. Her hands were clasped behind her head, lost in the tumbling curls of a vast blond mane; a tall, frosted glass of some tropical-looking drink stood improbably balanced on her perfectly flat stomach.

"I would kill for a body like that," the plump girl said, sighing.

"So would she, I bet." Claire hadn't meant to say it out loud. The words had just slipped out as she thought them, and the two girls turned to stare at her.

"What?" the thin girl asked.

Claire hesitated, and then decided that she might as well continue. "Come on, that's obviously trick photography," she said, pointing. "*Nobody* looks like that. The model's image has likely been digitally altered, and the glass was added in afterwards. And I bet the hair's a wig, too."

The plump girl's green-grey eyes looked resentfully at Claire through their pale lashes. "You think you know everything, don't you? You're probably just jealous," the girl accused, and she and her friend went back to gazing glumly at the ad.

Claire shrugged her shoulders and went back to her rummaging. On the other side of her locker, Mimi Taylor and her two best friends were talking. They were almost always talking, even in class. Both of Mimi's friends were named Chelsea; she called one of them Chel to avoid confusion, but Claire could never remember which one it was and mentally referred to the redhead as Chelsea One and the blonde as Chelsea Two. Collectively, she thought of them as Mimi and the Chelseas, as if they were some kind of girl band. They were, in fact, something of an ensemble: you almost never saw one of them without the other two, though Mimi was their unacknowledged leader.

There were two main groups in any school, Claire reflected, and they were separated by a kind of invisible barrier. Claire was undeniably a member of the "out" group and had accepted this without regret a long time ago. Mimi

& Co. were just as undeniably "in." Though they did not move in the upper stratosphere of the school's power cliques, they claimed their status by always knowing what was trendy and what was not. Whether it was nail polish with glitter, cute little stuffed animals attached to the shoulder straps of backpacks, or boy bands whose members all seemed to be named Jason, Jordan, or Justin, somehow they always *knew*. Invisible antennae reached out from their heads into some strange ethereal energy current to channel the latest fad. Today Mimi was dressed in a tight jersey top in swimming-pool blue and black jeans, and her dark squiggly hair was pulled off her face with a huge blue plastic clip. Outfit and accessories were the latest word in fashion. They had to be, or Mimi would die before she'd wear them.

"I tried this new one at the dance last night," Mimi was saying to her followers. "It's called Pink Dreams, and it is so cool. When I took it, I felt, like, totally blissed, and it lasted for hours. When I was on it, I just loved everybody."

She needed a drug for that? thought Claire irritably. *If anything, it should be the other way around. Loving Mimi Taylor would definitely require the ingestion of some mind-altering substance.*

"Of course, *some* people would be too goody-goody to take a little pill," the girl added, rolling her large violet eyes in Claire's direction.

"Yeah, why don't you do anything, Claire?" asked Chelsea Two. "Are you scared?"

"No," said Claire shortly. She unearthed her textbook at last and reached for her padlock, balancing the book on her forearm.

"I can get you some stuff to try," offered Chelsea One. "I know a good dealer. It'd be quality stuff, and safe, I promise."

"Why the pressure?" snapped Claire. "Do you get a commission?"

The red-headed girl recoiled. "Geez. I was just trying to be nice."

"Oh, never mind *her*," said Mimi in a bored voice. "She's always like that. C'mon, we're late for class."

Claire bit her lip to keep herself from retorting. She banged her locker door shut and snicked the padlock in place. It was partly her own fault, she grudgingly admitted. These days, she always felt as though she was covered in prickly spines, like a porcupine or a sea urchin; even when the spines were not raised in angry, bristling defence, they were always there, tense and ready. But knowing she was partly to blame did not improve her mood. *That's it,* she thought. *The very next person who rubs me the wrong way is going to wish she'd never—*

A hand came down on her shoulder, and she whirled around.

"Whoa!" Mrs. Robertson, the school guidance counsellor, held up her hands in a gesture of mock alarm. "Don't look so fierce, Claire. It's only me."

"Sorry," Claire apologized. She liked Mrs. Robertson, who had been patient and kind when Claire went through what she called her "rough patch" last year. As always, the woman was beautifully dressed—not with Mimi's obsessive attention to fashion, but with a classic, casual elegance. Her suit was a warm ochre hue, which harmonized with the dark brown of her skin, and her earrings were thin gold hoops that exactly matched the bangles on her wrist. A gold-and-ochre scarf at her neck tied the whole outfit together. She smiled at Claire, and the latter felt her mental spines begin to settle back.

"I just wanted to remind you about the self-image seminar I'm putting on today after school," Mrs. Robertson said. "I know you didn't sign up for it, and to tell you the truth, I don't think you need to go. I know there've been some problems, but I really think you're one of the more well-balanced kids I've ever met."

"Thanks," mumbled Claire.

"I *am* concerned about some of the girls who are coming, though. It's not just that they have self-image problems—they may be reluctant to say anything in the discussion afterwards. And my guest speaker is . . . well, not used to teenagers, and she may find it awkward. Claire, could you possibly spare the time and join us? You're bright, and you can get the conversational ball rolling if the others freeze up. Will you consider it?"

Claire was fishing for an excuse when she suddenly remembered that Dad was going to be working late. She could not face the long hours alone in the house, the bleak silence, the emptiness. "Sure," she agreed quickly.

"Oh, you don't have to decide right away. Just think about it and let me know later."

"No, I'd like to come. Really." Claire had no trouble sounding sincere, and Mrs. Robertson looked pleased.

"Thanks! I'll see you there, then. Four o'clock in the library."

◊   ◊   ◊

There had been a time, Claire remembered, when she was glad to go home after school. When she had run in her eagerness to get back to her room, her books and her computer . . . and Mom. She no longer felt a sharp pain when she thought of Mom, just a sort of dull, miserable ache. She had so enjoyed telling her mother about school: letting it all spill out, both the high and the low points of the day. It had helped to talk everything out with her and place it all in perspective. Now there was only the silence of the empty house before Dad came home from work—and even when he was there, he was usually too tired to talk or to listen.

She leaned on the sink, staring gloomily at her reflection in the washroom mirror. Her hair was the shade people call ash blond when they are being polite and dishwater blond when they aren't. Thick and frizzy and unruly, it bushed out around her rather square face and high forehead. Behind her glasses, with their unfashionably large lenses and dark heavy frames, her eyes were grey and wide-set. She certainly didn't look much like her mother. Mom's fair hair had been as smooth as silk and a pretty shade of pale gold; she had always worn it neatly pulled back in a hair clip or a patterned scarf. Though she was not conventionally pretty, her pronounced cheekbones and rather high-bridged nose gave her an elegant and well-bred look, like a minor member of some obscure European royal family.

Already the memory was fading around the edges, perhaps because of the move. Changing houses had relegated her mother to the past, Claire thought. She had been bitterly opposed to moving: she'd felt that her father was deliberately removing every last trace of Mom from their lives. The rooms that were still full of memories of her, the wallpapers she'd chosen, the flower bed out front that she'd lovingly tended, even the bits of junk mail that still arrived with her name on them—abandoning these things was like a rejection, like saying she wouldn't ever come back.

But moving house had not really changed everything. The old familiar rooms were gone, and with them Claire's half-conscious expectation of turning a corner and seeing her mother. But there were still the antique furnishings and draperies and other bits of decor that Mom had chosen, that they had kept in spite of everything. She followed them, haunted them like a lingering ghost . . .

There she went again, thinking of Mom as though she were dead.

The fact that the letters had stopped coming, that she'd missed Claire's last birthday, meant nothing. She had probably just forgotten. But this thought was not especially comforting either. *If she loves me, she's not alive. If she's alive, she doesn't love me.* These two thoughts had been whirling through Claire's brain for the past six months, endlessly tormenting her. They were with her when she woke up every morning, when she was trying to concentrate in class, when she came home at the end of the day. They were with her now as she strode down the hallway and pushed open the door of the library.

There were about eight or nine girls present, in addition to Mrs. Robertson and the guest speaker, a short little woman with untidy grey-brown hair wisping out of a bun and an ill-fitting beige pantsuit. Someone had set up some rows of plastic chairs in the open central area of the library, with a wooden podium and chair for the speaker in front. Claire sat down in the front row, glancing around her. Mimi and the Chelseas were here, to her surprise. What on earth were *they* doing in a seminar about positive self-image? They were attractive enough—and quite stuck on themselves, from what Claire could see. The pale, plump girl from the next-door locker and her slight, bespectacled friend were also present. Hopefully they at least would get some good out of this session.

Mrs. Robertson turned to face the seated girls and smiled her wide, radiant smile. "Hello, everyone! I'm glad to see you all here. I'd like to introduce our guest, Myra Moore. She's a very good friend of mine, and she'll be leading our seminar."

"Uh . . . hello," the older woman said. She did not seem to be nervous, Claire thought, just a bit vague, as though she was wondering how she could have ended up here, in the library of Willowville High. She cleared her throat, adjusted her glasses, fiddled with her notes on the podium, and finally said, "I wonder, Pam, if we could rearrange all these chairs? Into a circle, perhaps? It'd look a little less . . . well, authoritative and hierarchical."

"Whatever you like, Myra," replied Mrs. Robertson in her smooth-as-coffee voice. They all got up and rearranged the rows of plastic chairs into a roughly circular formation. Mrs. Moore moved her own chair into it as well.

"There, that's better!" she said. The vagueness had gone, and Claire noticed that she had left her notes on the podium. "Now we're all on an equal footing, no one set above anyone else. And we can all see each other's faces, too. Circular seating arrangements are very old, when you think about it. They go back to the ancient tribespeople, the hunters and gatherers sitting in a ring around their camp-fires. Imagine that we're people from long ago, with a big fire burning there in the centre, where the carpet is. We'd be listening to a storyteller, perhaps—and maybe there'd be a witch doctor or a wise woman. We're not telling stories today, unfortunately, though I hope you'll find what I have to say interesting."

The girls shifted restlessly on the hard plastic seats, their eyes drifting somewhat. Mimi and the Chelseas seemed particularly uncomfortable: they had at first taken seats in the back row of chairs, no doubt intending to chatter as usual, and now found themselves exposed to the gaze of everyone in the circle.

The guest speaker continued: "Before we get into the bit about body images and so on, I'd like us to look at some common words and terms. I'm thinking specifically of gender-oriented put-downs, and whether it's possible to rehabilitate some of the words used. What negative words can you think of that are used for women today? Have you ever been called a witch, for instance?" One or two heads nodded, and there were some embarrassed titters. "What other insults are used for girls only?"

There was a long pause. "Come on, girls," urged Mrs. Robertson, leaning forward with an encouraging smile. "You can think of some. There's that little word that rhymes with 'witch.' I've been overhearing it quite a lot in the hallways." The girls looked at each other and giggled.

Claire remembered that she was supposed to be helping with the discussion. "Yes, and the word some men use for an unattractive woman is 'dog,'" she commented.

"True. I've often wondered why the word 'dog' is used in such a negative way," mused Mrs. Moore. "I mean, dogs are beautiful creatures, and very loving and loyal, and so many other nice things. Why should 'dog' be an insult? If anything, it's a compliment."

"A lot of words used on women are animal words, aren't they?" the guidance counsellor said. "I remember that you made up quite a list of them at one seminar, Myra. Shrew, chick, bat, barracuda. Can anyone think of any others?" She looked around the circle.

"Cow," said one girl, grinning.

"Now that one is interesting," remarked Mrs. Moore. "You see, cows are sacred in many cultures. In India, for instance. If you ever visit Calcutta, you'll see sacred cattle wandering freely through the streets. And the ancient Egyptians had a goddess, Hathor, who took the shape of a cow."

"What other animal insults can you girls think of?" prompted Mrs. Robertson.

"Sometimes when we think a girl's, you know, acting mean or something, we make mewing sounds at her," said another girl.

Mrs. Moore laughed. "Yes, and did you know that the cat was a sacred animal, too? The Egyptians had a cat goddess named Bast who was the protector of women. But cats were also associated with witches in medieval Europe. You've all seen those scary-looking black cats on Halloween decorations. Witches were supposed to have things called familiars, demon companions that took the forms of cats. Why was all this animal imagery attached to women, you may ask? Well, you see, in the old patriarchal belief systems, women were always linked to nature. Heaven was seen as the abode of a male god, the model for all male rulers on earth below. So men in those days saw themselves as the champions of goodness and order and civilization. The natural world, on the other hand, was *dis*orderly: scary and uncontrollable and chaotic. These men saw it as a threat. And they felt that women were somehow closer to this puzzling realm of nature than to civilization and order. Their ability to give birth, for instance, must have made them seem mysterious. And things we don't understand can be frightening. I believe that's where all these animal-based insults come from: a deep sense of fear and uncertainty. Personally, I love animals, and I think the natural world is beautiful and fascinating."

Heads nodded in agreement all around the circle.

"I see you do, too. I'm glad, because that's something we as a society need to do: reaffirm the goodness of nature, of our environment. So much for natural images of women. What about supernatural images? We've dealt with the word 'witch' already. But there are others. Women who are considered too strong, too pushy, are called dragons, harpies, basilisks, banshees, or hags. All of these are mythical creatures, but they're still associated with the destructive powers of nature. Dragons were often connected to such natural phenomena as earthquakes, floods, and whirlwinds. Harpies are half woman, half bird of prey; banshees are fairy women, and fairies symbolize the mystery of the natural world.

"What these images tell me is that men who use them are afraid of unfettered female power. And women who use them on other women are afraid of their own power. As little girls, we're taught that we must be sweet and gentle, and as a result, we're often afraid to appear otherwise. Not too long ago, girls were also instructed to be submissive. In other words, we're supposed to be feminine. Women and girls who step outside this boundary are feared and frowned upon, even today."

She talked on for a little while, about how women are portrayed in the mass media and in advertising, about the ways women view themselves and the need for self-esteem and strong role models. She discussed ideal body weights for women and how these had changed over the centuries, and Mrs. Robertson added a few more comments about eating disorders. Finally, Mrs. Moore asked if there were any questions. Claire had readied a rather obvious one about artificially altered body images (remembering the magazine ad on the locker door), just in case no one had anything to ask. But quite a few of the girls had questions, including the pale, plump girl—whose name, Claire now learned, was Donna Reese. Her friend was named Linda Kwan, and she, too, wanted to talk about her own image problems, and her shyness evaporated as she spoke.

Mimi suddenly stuck up her hand. "Are you going to talk some more about witches? Not just insults, I mean, but the real kind?"

"Real kind?" repeated Mrs. Moore, looking blank.

"Real witches. You are one, aren't you?"

There was a silence. "Me?" Mrs. Moore looked startled. "I don't . . . At least I . . . Wherever did you . . . ?" she stammered and then fell silent, throwing a helpless glance at Mrs. Robertson.

The guidance counsellor's smooth, rich voice immediately poured into the gap. "I don't think we'll get into that just now, Mimi. Are there any other questions?"

No one else had anything to say. Most of the girls, including Claire, were staring at Mimi, who seemed oblivious to the sensation she had created. What was all that about witches? Had the girl finally fried her brains? But Mrs. Moore had seemed so flustered. And that quick intervention by Mrs. Robertson was odd, too—almost as if she were covering up for something.

Mrs. Moore stood. "Now, if you don't mind, I'm going to ask you all to do something extremely corny. Would you please stand up and hold each other's hands? And shut your eyes."

Startled, they obeyed without a murmur. "All right," said Mrs. Moore's voice, "I'd like you to just be quiet for a moment and *feel* this circle—feel the hands to either side of you, joining you to your two neighbours. Imagine that you're joined to everyone else in the circle through them—that a kind of energy is flowing through it, around and around, linking us, making us one whole. Let's be quiet a moment and just listen to ourselves breathing."

Silence fell. One girl tittered but quickly stopped. There was nothing but the warmth of the others' hands, the quiet and the stillness. Claire heard the gentle rise and fall of breathing all around her, the low drone of the school's heating system, traffic sounds far away on the main road. It was rather peaceful and calming.

"There!" Mrs. Moore said abruptly, breaking the mood. They dropped each other's hands and looked at her. "Now, I'd like to thank you all for coming today, and I know you're all just dying to run back home and hit the books." The girls laughed, and the circle broke up.

Claire stayed behind to help Mrs. Robertson put the chairs away. The guidance counsellor thanked her again for showing up.

"I didn't mind; it was interesting. The other girls did all right without me, actually," Claire remarked.

"Yes, I was pleasantly surprised. But thanks anyway, Claire. I have to run now. I'll call you later in the week, Myra." With a last wave, Mrs. Robertson strode briskly from the room.

The older woman was standing at the podium, shoving her unused notes into a worn old briefcase. "Yes, that went rather well," she observed to Claire. "I'm not a very good speaker, I'm afraid."

"You were fine," Claire reassured her.

"I only hope I've done some good." Mrs. Moore sighed,
"It's so hard for you young girls nowadays—though it never
was easy in any age, I suppose." Then she glanced up at
Claire as though she were really seeing her for the first time.
"You poor dear!" she exclaimed.

It was so unusual to hear those words without the custom-
ary sarcastic inflection that Claire was taken aback. "I . . . I
beg your pardon?" she murmured.

"Don't worry. Your mother is safe." Mrs. Moore laid a
hand on Claire's shoulder, then blinked once or twice as
though she herself was unsure why she had spoken.

"You know my mom?" Claire burst out.

The little woman looked confused. She blinked again, ran
an unsteady hand through her untidy hair, and murmured,
"Why, no. I don't know her. I'm sorry, I shouldn't have said
that."

"But—"

"I really must be off!" Mrs. Moore hefted her battered
briefcase and almost scuttled out of the room, leaving Claire
to stare after her in bewilderment.

What did she mean? Why did she say that?

Chapter 2

IT WAS CLOSE TO FIVE O'CLOCK when Claire took the 12A bus home. As she stood in the shelter, she saw Mimi Taylor roar past in her lipstick red car, followed by Chelsea Two in her second-hand BMW. Other kids had cars, Claire reflected in discontent. She still hadn't even taken a driving lesson: there was no money for the fee right now, Dad said, so she had to ride her bike or take the bus. It was a long ride, as the bus's route wove in and out of the central Willowville suburbs before heading along Lakeside Boulevard to the downtown area.

Despite its name, Lakeside did not actually give a view of the shore of Lake Ontario: there were large, stately properties on both sides of the boulevard, expensive Georgian- or Victorian-style houses on spacious lots. Their lawns were well manicured, with the occasional ornamental flower bed, impatiens and petunias still flaunting their vivid summer colours in the September sun. Those on the side facing the lake, with a view of its vast blue expanse, were of course the most expensive; some were a century old or more, like the historic Glengarry estate, which had been turned into a public park and museum. The larger estates were surrounded by tall fences of iron railings or by stone walls, and they had grand gated entrances, some with concrete urns or lamps atop stone posts. There were two estates in particular that had enchanted Claire from her early childhood days, when she and her mother drove past them on the way to the farmer's market at the eastern end of town. One, surrounded by an iron fence, contained a beautiful old house with a small orchard whose apple trees flowered in pink and white every spring. *Had* flowered. They were all gone now—chopped down to make way for a small housing development—and the old house had also been razed.

"You can't blame the heirs for selling these places off," Dad had said. "Properties that size belong to another era: they cost a lot to maintain, and the taxes are extortionate."

Claire had conceded his point. But she still felt a little twinge of hostility whenever she passed the new development inside the iron fence. The houses that had replaced the orchard were big, ugly things of sand-coloured brick, all crowded cheek by jowl on tiny lots to make the greatest use of the land. Though expensive, they were cheaply and badly made: the brick was fake, and Claire had heard that their inner walls were thin and their roofs prone to leakage. The house that had been built on the site of the old one was even larger and more hideous. Claire had watched resentfully as, little by little, its massive walls rose: grey walls of what looked like cinder blocks, topped by pretentious turrets. It looked like a Victorian prison, she thought, or a small

version of Dracula's Castle; she could not believe that
anyone would actually choose to live in such a place. But
apparently it had been designed and built to someone's
specifications. There had never been a For Sale sign out
front, and this morning, as the bus drove past, she had
noticed a large moving van parked in the ostentatious
circular driveway.

The estate shared a huge block, much larger than the
blocks in her more ordinary neighbourhood, with another
property. This second, separate estate was still as Claire
remembered it from her childhood. The same developer who
had ruined the property next door had tried hard to get his
hands on this one, too, but in vain: the old man who had
lived there would not sell. He had died this year, though, at
the ripe old age of ninety-two, and she waited in dread for
his heirs to sell and the inevitable development sign to
appear.

The estate, called Willowmere, was her favourite and
always had been. Its outer wall was of stone topped by iron
railings, and there were lions on its gateposts—not little
concrete ones like those you sometimes saw in front of
suburban homes, but big, grey stone ones with regal crowns
on their heads, obviously very old. Sometimes the gate was
left open, so she could catch tantalizing glimpses of the
grounds within as she rode by in a bus or car. There were
cedar trees and yew hedges, some of the latter clipped into
fanciful shapes, and green lawns and some statuary she
could see fleetingly: there was a dark green shape that
looked like a seated Buddha and, farther on, a small summer
house with a pagoda roof. That was all she could ever see
before the walls once more hid it all from view. A cedar
hedge grew behind the railings, shielding the property from

curious eyes. But Claire had once or twice come here on her bike and peeked through the curtain of close-growing cedars at enchanting vistas of the grounds beyond. There was a small stream meandering under a grove of gnarled old willows, with little arched Oriental bridges crossing it here and there, and a pair of bronze Japanese cranes wading in mid-current. Part of the stream had been diverted to make a wide, shallow pool, out of which rose a fountain—not a little, suburban-style fountain, but a large one such as you might see in a public park sending up a majestic three-metre jet of spray. She had stared at this in utter amazement when she first glimpsed it through the hedge. Imagine having a fountain like that in your *backyard!*

The house, unlike the gardens, could be seen easily from the road. It was hard to miss, in fact, for the red brick building was nearly as large as the one she called Dracula's Castle and also sported a conical turret, as well as a number of gables and a widow's walk. But this old house did not look pretentious, even with the turret. It was whimsical, like a man wearing a funny hat to amuse some children. Its bizarre mix of architectural styles was self-consciously witty, as though the house did not take itself at all seriously. Even the elaborate gingerbread trim that ran around the eaves seemed humorous. At Halloween, it was done up as a wonderful haunted house, with bedsheet ghosts and fake cobwebs hanging in swags over the porch, and not one or two but a whole trail of jack-o'-lanterns leading all the way up the winding path, their carved faces mischievously glowing. And at Christmas there were multi-coloured lights strung everywhere, all around the gingerbread eaves and gables of the house, and the pagoda summer house was lit up too.

It was, she thought, a friendly place, and when she was a little girl she used to imagine herself living there. Sometimes she saw herself as a grown-up married woman with a large family; sometimes she lived there all alone. Always she had lots of pets: cats and dogs and hamsters and fish, and a talking parrot that rode around on her shoulder, with perhaps a pony or a pet llama in a stable out back and peacocks strutting everywhere. Bit by bit, she had furnished the imagined interior with things that she had admired in magazines or store windows: tables with legs ending in lion paws; Tiffany lamps; one or two interesting paintings that had caught her eye. The room in the turret was, of course, her private study. It had a stained-glass window, she knew, because she had seen the lovely jewel colours glowing through the dark once when she passed it after sundown. The old house became a place that she retreated to more and more often as time went by.

She gazed at the Willowmere estate in longing as the bus passed it. Then the vulgar grey house with the turrets came into view. The moving van was still in the driveway. There was also a black, shiny, low-slung sports car parked near the front door, and an arrogant-looking young man, tall and dark-haired—no doubt the owner of the car and the house—stood by the moving van, directing the workmen with sweeping, self-important arm gestures. She found herself hating him, even at that distance.

The bus rumbled on into the downtown core, and Claire glanced at her watch. Five-thirty. Dad wouldn't be back for an hour at least, and dinner would be something instant, as usual. There was time to get off at the downtown stop and go to the bookstore, then walk the rest of the way home. Claire reached up, tugged on the cord to make the Stop

Requested sign flash on, and shouldered her backpack as the bus obediently rolled to a halt.

She walked along in the wan golden light, past the storefronts. It was Friday, so most places were still open. Past the Pick of the Litter pet store she walked, the Lakeside Pharmacy, Marie's Boutique, and the Sidewalk Café to the new store that had just opened at the end of the block.

Claire's favourite bookstore, the Book Nook, had recently merged with another local store, a New Age establishment called the Magick Shoppe. Neither had been making much of a go of it lately. Old Mr. Brown, the proprietor of the Book Nook, had faced strong competition from some big bookstore chains, and the Magick Shoppe had not been able to find the right clientele in conservative suburban Willowville: most people seemed to think that it supplied party tricks to professional magicians. The new combined store, renamed Books & Magic, had opened its doors for business the previous weekend.

Claire had never ventured into the Magick Shoppe, and she looked now with distaste at the display of quartz crystals, tarot cards, and pewter pixies in the window of Books & Magic. As she opened the door, she was hit by a wave of Oriental incense, along with a blast of Celtic folk music. On the new bulletin board by the cash desk were promotional flyers for various events, from a workshop on channelling (to put you in touch with your spirit guide), to a seminar on aura photography and chakra analysis, to a lecture by someone who would interpret your dreams for a fee. Claire groaned and turned away.

At least the long aisles of ancient, book-crammed shelves were still there. And old Mr. Brown was still behind the desk, wearing his usual dour expression. She smiled and greeted him cheerily. He was not as formidable as he seemed, and she had become quite good friends with him over the years. He had recommended some very good books, many of which had gone on to become her favourites. One of her guilty indulgences was fantasy fiction. She always carefully hid her new purchases, with their bright, garish covers, from her father's disapproving eyes. He would prefer that she read something more educational, she knew, something to improve the mind; but the books gave her a much-needed escape.

One day, she had been hesitating between a couple of books—the cover of one showed a sword-wielding hero battling a three-headed dragon, the other depicted a princess in a flowing gown riding a flying horse—when Mr. Brown had approached her and gently but firmly placed in her hand a book with a single glaring red eye on its cover. "If you're going to read fantasy," he said in his gruff voice, "read the good stuff." She obediently bought the book. It was Tolkien's *Fellowship of the Ring,* the first in the Lord of the Rings trilogy; she had never quite felt up to tackling that monumental work, but after reading the first volume, she had dashed back to the store to buy the other two. For weeks afterwards, she had daydreamed about being Lady Eowyn, fearlessly facing down the Dark Lord's minions.

"How's it going?" she asked Mr. Brown as she passed the cash desk.

"We're managing. No major fights yet. At least I got them to take the *K* off 'magic,'" he muttered. "Abominable affectation."

He seemed even grumpier than usual, though Claire didn't altogether blame him. She went over to the book-shelves and perused them. So many fantasies these days seemed to be about some young girl who served the Great Goddess but was persecuted by an evil patriarchal society and forced to flee into the wilderness, where she learned about magic from the earth spirits. Claire had read several novels of this type and quite enjoyed them at first, but she was beginning to find the plots repetitive. Besides, magic was boring when you really thought about it. Where was the suspense when the protagonist could just snap her fingers and teleport herself out of danger?

She gave up on the fantasy section and turned to some non-fiction books tidily arranged on an adjacent table. A few were propped up to display their covers. One was titled *Secrets of Stonehenge: The Ancient Knowledge of the Druids Revealed*. Claire snorted. Oh, please! The Druids didn't build Stonehenge. It was made back in Neolithic times by people no one knows anything about. Not much was known about the Druids either, come to that. How could this author claim to know about their ancient beliefs when the Druids never wrote anything down? Another book was about UFOs. *Yup, that's right,* Claire thought. *Extraterrestrials who travel thousands of light-years to abduct rural housewives and make pretty patterns in farmers' fields.* "Are we being visited by intelligent beings from alien worlds?" the dust jacket asked. *If we are, I sure wouldn't call them intelligent.*

Claire glanced at the book next to it, and her eyes focused sharply on the author's name: Dr. Myra Moore, Ph.D. Coincidence, she told herself; Myra Moore must be a very common name. But she couldn't help picking it up and glancing at the back cover. And there was the face, spectacles and wispy hair and all, of the woman from the school workshop. *She never told us she had a doctorate,* Claire thought, and she felt an increase of respect for Myra Moore. The book was called *A Journey through Gaia,* and Dr. Moore seemed to be a combination of naturalist and travel writer, according to the jacket copy, which included a quote from a prominent journalist. "This incredible woman has trekked through the equatorial rainforest, gone dog sledding in the High Arctic, swum with humpback whales and listened to their songs echo through the deep," he said. "As a young woman, she once got lost in the jungles of Guatemala, eventually wandering into a small, isolated village whose inhabitants took her for an apparition of the Virgin. If there's anything Myra Moore hasn't done, it's not worth doing."

Claire flipped through the pages, reading bits at random. There were lots of photographs: in one a much younger Myra Moore, dressed in shorts and a pith helmet, was riding a camel across the desert; in another she was surrounded by grinning pygmies in an African forest; still another showed her in scuba gear, preparing to jump over the side of a boat. She had certainly had a remarkable life.

Then another photograph caught Claire's eye. It was an outdoor gathering of some rather hairy and hippie-ish individuals, dressed in what looked like medieval cloaks and robes. Myra stood in the centre of the group. The caption explained that this was a gathering of Wiccans, or modern-day witches, in California, adding that Myra Moore had been "involved" with the movement for some years.

Wiccans. Modern witches.

So despite her denials at the seminar, Myra Moore *was* a witch, of a kind anyway. Mimi had evidently learned of this somehow—though why trendy Mimi should be interested in some obscure branch of the occult was anybody's guess.

Claire gave a little shrug and put the book back on the display table. Then she suddenly remembered Myra's odd little comment about her mother and froze with her hand still on the book.

Could it be . . . ? Mom had joined some kind of New Age movement before she left, Dad said. Did Myra know Mom after all? Had the woman promised not to tell anyone about Mom and then made a slip of the tongue? And was that why she'd looked so confused and guilty before hastening from the room? Claire looked up from the book table feeling dazed. How long had she been standing here? Mr. Brown was gone from the counter, replaced by a tall, thin girl in a clingy black dress, and the Celtic music had given way to chanting Tibetan monks. Claire headed for the door and home, still feeling light-headed.

What does Myra Moore know? How can I find her and make her tell me?

◆   ◆   ◆

When she arrived home, the front porch light was on and the door unlocked. Good, Dad was back. That meant she wouldn't have to arrange dinner. Not that it would be anything special. The two of them had subsisted mainly on frozen and instant dinners ever since Mom left. Mom had hated cooking as much as Claire and her father did, but unlike them, she had actually been good at it. Claire had not attempted to recreate any of her mouth-watering casseroles and desserts—the memories they evoked still hurt too much—though she could make lasagna and a passable chicken cacciatore. But most nights, she didn't feel like cooking from scratch.

The microwave was going and the heavy, moist smell of instant pasta wafted towards her as she entered the small kitchen. Her father was sitting at the table, working away on a calculator and surrounded by bills. His expression was glum.

"So are we broke yet?" Claire asked lightly, tossing her backpack into a chair and moving to look over his shoulder. He just grunted. "Maybe I could get a job," she suggested. "That might help."

"That's not necessary," he replied, taking off his glasses and rubbing his eyes.

"It's not just general expenses," she said. "I'd like more pocket money."

He glanced up, frowning slightly. "I'll give you money. I'll give you anything you want—just ask me."

She bit her lip. She didn't want to seem ungrateful, but . . . "Dad, I'm sixteen now. I don't want to be given things. I want to buy them, with money I've *earned*."

He put his glasses back on and returned to his calculations. "You know, financial independence is a wonderful thing," he remarked, "and I'm glad you take it seriously. But it comes along with a bunch of other things, like bills and taxes and mortgage rates and rent. There's a very good reason why you don't see any adults skipping around saying, 'Whee, I'm a wage earner! I'm having so much fun!'"

"And people wonder where I get my sarcastic tongue from," Claire said, slumping into a chair opposite his.

He pushed the calculator aside. "Listen, Claire, you've got a good mind, and you can probably do just about anything you want when you graduate. I'd rather you spent your time studying instead of preparing fast food or slaving away behind a sales counter just so you can buy all kinds of clothes and gadgets that will be obsolete a year from now.

And sleeping through your classes because you're too dog-tired to concentrate. Right now your work is school, and I'd prefer that you focus on it. You can work in the summer if you like; during the school year, I'll provide for all your needs, at least till you graduate. Deal?"

"Okay." Claire shrugged. "Well, if we're not too broke, could I have a pet? A cat maybe, or a dog?"

A little silence fell. They were both trying not to think of the old family cat, Whiskers. He really had been like a member of the family, for he had been slightly older than Claire herself. He'd turned up on the doorstep as a stray kitten shortly after Mom and Dad married. Then a few years ago, he had not come in one evening when he was called. Mom had gone out and seen Whiskers lying in the grass, bleeding from a terrible wound, and a large, dark animal—a dog, she thought, or possibly a coyote—leaping away over the back fence. The vet had not been able to save Whiskers, and Mom had been distraught. It was the cat's death, Claire thought, that had somehow started off the whole miserable chain of change. Life was never the same again afterwards.

"It'd be nice to have something to greet me when I come home after school," she said now, breaking the silence. "And to keep me company when you're away." Claire's father worked for a computer software company, and he had to make frequent business trips to trade shows and conventions. Claire found the days of solitude when he was away almost unbearable.

Her father rubbed his eyes again. "We'll see."

"Dad, you always say that. Why couldn't we have a pet?"

"Well, if you're thinking of a puppy, it'll need a lot of care. Housebreaking and all that. And the poor mutt would be alone all day, five days a week."

"So we'll get a cat, then. They don't mind being alone, and they're not too expensive to keep either."

"We'll see," he said again.

He didn't say, "Cats remind me too much of your mother." But Claire was sure that was what was going through his mind. Why else would he hesitate? She gave it up. There was no point in starting another argument. He looked tired and harassed, and suddenly she knew she couldn't broach the subject of Myra and what she'd said about Mom. Not tonight, and perhaps not ever. She would have to pursue the matter on her own.

I'll just have to get hold of that Moore woman and find out what she knows, she thought. *Much more than she was willing to tell me today, I'm sure.*

Behind them, the microwave pinged. "That one can be yours," Dad said without looking up. "Put another dinner in for me, will you?"

"Okay."

CHAPTER 3

CLAIRE HAD INTENDED at first to approach Mrs. Robertson and try to get Dr. Moore's phone number from her. But she felt reluctant to do so when she went to school the next day. It might only result in more counselling, she thought with a grimace; the guidance counsellor had advised her to try to get on with her life and allow Mom to get on with hers. "She's started a new phase, a new existence," the counsellor had explained carefully. "I know you don't agree with that, and I don't say you have to, but I'm afraid you will have to accept it as reality for now." If Claire asked for the number and Mrs. Robertson asked the reason for her request, she would have to tell her. She could not lie to Pam Robertson.

I'd have to tell her the whole story, and she'd think I'm backsliding. And I'm not, Claire insisted to herself. *I'm not trying to get Mom back. I just want to know how she is.*

So she stayed away from Mrs. Robertson. But she could not forget the odd look on Dr. Moore's face when she had said, "Your mother is safe." She decided to approach Mimi Taylor between classes, when they were both at their lockers.

"Hey, Mimi," she said, "how'd you know that Moore woman was into witchcraft?"

Mimi gave a little indifferent shrug. "There are some kids here at school who are into Wicca, and they mentioned Myra. Sometimes she has witches' gatherings at her place. There was one last night, and my friends and I went along just to see what it was like."

"I never knew anything about Wicca before," put in Chelsea One, arriving at her own locker with Chelsea Two. "I didn't realize how popular it is."

"It's popular?" asked Claire, surprised.

The redhead nodded. "Yeah, totally. All the cool people are into it; they get together and do magic circles and spells and stuff."

So that explained why Mimi and the Chelseas had gone to Myra's workshop. If witchcraft was "cool," then of course they had to do it; hence the attempt to pump Dr. Moore for more information—until Mrs. Robertson intervened. Talking about witchcraft on the school premises would be a definite no-no. Undeterred, they'd gone and got themselves invited to the witches' gathering.

"So what did they do—Dr. Moore's friends, I mean?"

"They danced around in a circle and chanted," Chelsea One replied. "At least, the adults did; the rest of us were only allowed to watch. They did it outdoors 'cause it was so nice out. They called it a *sabbat*—that's a sort of holiday. It was to celebrate the autumn equinox, they said, and the end of the growing season and all that. They call their group the Starwind Coven. Isn't that a great name?"

Mimi snorted. "It wasn't that great. Catch me going to one of those *sabbat* things again! I asked and asked, and none of them would tell me how to make a love potion."

Claire stared at her. "What do you mean, a love potion? Like in a fairy tale?"

"I mean, like, if you really, really want some guy to love you, and he doesn't, how do you *make* him?"

"They said they can't do that," Chelsea One explained. "They have charms to, like, summon romance into your life. But they can't *make* a person fall in love with you."

Mimi shrugged. "I guess that's true. I thought at first they were holding out on me, but now I think those Wiccans really don't know squat about love spells. It figures. They were just a bunch of total granolas anyway."

"A bunch of what?" asked Claire.

"Oh, you know the type. Wholesome and all-natural. They were mostly older, and almost all of them had long hair—even some of the guys—and they had these hokey, made-up names, like Greywolf and Ravenwing. And they prayed to the Earth Mother. It was, like, so 1960s. But I guess that wouldn't bother someone like you," she added, as though suddenly remembering that she was, after all, talking to a member of the "not in" crowd.

"Well, if they can't tell us how to do a love potion, we'll just have to find someone else who can," Chelsea Two said. "I'd really like to use one on Dave Nielsen. He is a total hunk! There's a girl in my social-studies class who says she can do spells and stuff. Josie Sloan. We can ask her."

The Wiccans could say what they liked, Claire thought in sudden irritation. For her own part, she firmly believed in the Devil. Who else, after all, would have arranged for her locker to be right next to Mimi Taylor's? But she restrained the sharp comments she longed to make and turned to Chelsea One. "Do you happen to have Dr. Moore's address or phone number, then?" she asked, in as casual a tone as she could manage. "You never know, I might want to check out this Wicca thing sometime."

"Yeah, sure." Chelsea One reached into her backpack and brought out a small address book. She read out a phone number, and Claire jotted it in a margin of her math notebook. It would be an easy matter to look up the address in the phone book. Thanking the girl, she headed off to class feeling better than she had in some days. She was still not sure if she was actually going to confront Dr. Moore or not.

But at least she would know where to find her.

✧   ✧   ✧

Claire dithered for the rest of the week, picking the phone up and putting it down again, debating whether to tell her father or Mrs. Robertson. If she'd only had a best friend to confide in, someone her own age to share her plan with, it might have helped her come to a decision. But Claire had had no friends for some years now. Her former best friend, a girl named Ainsley who had lived on the same street, had moved with her family to another city a few years before Claire's mother left. And after that, Claire had been too depressed to seek out any new friendships.

Claire finally set out on her bike Saturday morning, early but not too early, with Dr. Moore's address in her backpack. The streets were quiet as she cycled along, most people sleeping in or enjoying their day off. Perhaps she should have phoned Dr. Moore first, to make sure she wasn't sleeping in too. But Claire wanted to confront the woman face to face.

Why hadn't she told Claire more, explained how she knew her mother and how she could be certain that Mom was all right? Claire wanted to demand these things, watching Dr. Moore's expression for any sign of shame or guilt. A phone call would not show her this, and to call in advance of her visit would give Dr. Moore a chance to compose herself, to come up with a plausible explanation. Much better to catch her off guard.

I'm getting paranoid, Claire thought. But she cycled on, determinedly.

The address, according to the phone directory, was 321 Lakeside Boulevard, which meant that Dr. Moore's house was about halfway along the road and on the south side. There were quite a few smaller houses in that area, most built on the sites of former estates or constructed in past decades when smaller homes were the fashion. Claire cycled down to the foot of Birch, then crossed Lakeside and turned east along the bicycle path. The journey seemed much longer than it did when she went by bus. But the day was bright and clear and cool. She pedalled on, enjoying the sun and the breeze. 305 Lakeside, 307, 309—the numbers flicked past, carved on wooden signposts, displayed in cast iron over doorways. 311, 313, 315. The small houses with their well-kept front lawns streamed past. On her bike, down close to everything instead of watching from a bus window, Claire noticed so much more. Flowers in planters, lawn ornaments, toys children had left lying in driveways. She wondered what Dr. Moore's house was like. Old-fashioned, she thought, cottagey-looking, with painted shutters and perhaps a picket fence painted to match.

317 . . . She had come to the last of the houses on this block, a bungalow with a connected garage. Beyond lay a

beige brick wall: the new development, with the huge and hideous beige brick homes. But none of these faced on Lakeside. Instead, they faced each other in two long rows, and a new road had been put in between them, a short cul-de-sac grandly labelled "Lakeview Drive." She stopped pedalling and stared about her. But that must mean . . .

She cycled on, past the monstrous grey house with its Gothic turrets and circular driveway. 319 Lakeside. No, it couldn't be . . . She whizzed on, past stone walls and high hedges of cedar. There was the dunce-cap tower, there the walls of warm red brick rising beyond the shrubs. She came to the gate with the two crowned stone lions perching atop the posts, and there on one of the posts was a small brass plaque:

Willowmere
321 Lakeside Blvd.

"I don't believe it," said Claire aloud.

Of course she had never noticed the number. The plaque was so small, and whenever she'd passed the gate in a bus or car, she had been too preoccupied with stealing that fleeting peek at the grounds inside to pay any attention to the address. Here . . . Dr. Myra Moore lived here. *In my house,* thought Claire, for she still thought of it as somehow hers. *What a crazy* coincidence, part of her mind thought. But at the same instant, another part was saying, *This was meant to be.* At last . . . at last she would be able to enter that forbidden gate, to go past the notice that said Private and on into those enchanting grounds.

Her hands clenched on the handlebars of her bike. Then she slipped off the seat and wheeled it up the drive, past the gate and under the scowls of the stone lions. Up the long winding drive she went, feeling as though she had entered one of her own daydreams. There were the cedar trees, and there the seated Buddha, calmly meditating among the shrubbery. There was the summer house with the pagoda roof. And the fountain—as she walked past, she felt its fine spray on her cheek, blown towards her by the breeze off the lake. In the pool, large carp, some golden and some calico, idled to and fro. There were other things she'd never glimpsed before: a stone figure of a man in monk's attire surrounded by animals—St. Francis of Assisi, perhaps?— and lots of other statues, and a sundial, and a birdbath in which some sparrows were fluttering and quarrelling. There was an old greenhouse, no longer in use, and behind it a separate cottage that had to have been for a gardener, though it looked abandoned now. There were shrubs clipped into those elaborate pompom shapes that always reminded her of French poodles. And there before her eyes was the great house—so close!

She walked on in a sort of daze, past the poodle bushes and towards the house. Suddenly there was a volley of barks, and Claire tensed, expecting an enraged Doberman or a Rottweiler. Instead, a lovely collie with feathered legs and snowy ruff came running towards her.

"For heaven's sake, Angus MacTavish!" called a woman's voice. "What is it, another squirrel? Leave it alone, there's a good boy."

From behind a clump of shrubbery at the side of the house appeared a head topped by a broad-brimmed straw hat. It was Myra Moore. She was wearing some grubby old clothes and a pair of gardening gloves, and as Claire put down the kickstand of her bike and approached, feeling more than ever like an intruder, she saw a basket full of bulbs sitting on the ground. A fleeting memory came to her—of watching her mother plant tulip and daffodil bulbs in the fall—and it hardened her resolve to question the woman.

"The gate was open," she said, defending her trespass, "so I thought it would be okay to come in. I was wondering if you could help me with something."

Dr. Moore was peering at her in puzzlement. Then a light broke in her face. "Oh, it's you—the girl from the high-school discussion group," she said. "Claire Norton, isn't it? How can I help you, dear?" Despite her friendly tone, there was definitely a hint of embarrassment or unease in her manner.

Claire faced her directly. "Why did you say that about my mother being all right? You *do* know her, don't you?"

Now she saw, again, the guilty look in the woman's eyes. "I'm afraid not. I've never met your mother."

"So why did you say what you did?"

Dr. Moore looked small and contrite, kneeling there in the dirt—as though she, and not the trespasser Claire, was the guilty party. "Oh, dear! It was an impulse. I hope you don't mind, but Pam told me how your mother left you. And then when I saw that sad, worried look on your face, the words just popped out before I thought. I really don't know why I said them, and I shouldn't have. I am so very sorry."

Claire suddenly felt like a fool. Of course Mrs. Robertson had told her friend about Mrs. Norton. There was nothing confidential about the information: the departure of Claire Norton's mother was common knowledge at school, and Mrs. Robertson had likely let Dr. Moore know the awkward truth in advance so she wouldn't put her foot in her mouth when talking to Claire. After all, Claire had told the counsellor how sick she was of explaining to well-meaning inquirers that she had no mother at home. Why on earth hadn't she thought of this in the first place, instead of seeing sinister conspiracies everywhere?

She backed away, mumbling, "I . . . I just thought you might know her, and how she is. I haven't heard from her lately, and . . ."

Myra looked at her thoughtfully. "Claire, why don't you stay and have a hot cup of tea or something? Please do. You look a bit faint, and I feel just awful about this."

"It doesn't matter," Claire replied dully. "Just a misunderstanding, that's all. I don't want to interrupt your gardening."

Dr. Moore stood, brushing dirt off her knees. "No, I need to take a break. I get carried away when I'm gardening and lose track of time, and then I end up having a sore back for days afterwards. Do me a favour and stay. I've got some homemade muffins."

Claire hesitated. "Well . . . it's kind of you, Dr. Moore."

"Oh, do please call me Myra. 'Dr. Moore' always makes me feel like a character in a hospital drama."

Again Claire's mind was divided. Part of her wanted to go into the house, part hesitated. But Dr. Moore was already heading for the front porch with the dog at her heels. Claire had to follow her. She looked up at the turret, the gingerbread trim—now what did that make her think of? The gingerbread house from *Hansel and Gretel,* owned by the witch who ate children . . . No, that was silly.

As she walked towards the porch, Claire saw a big, blue-breasted bird come around the corner of the house, trailing a long, somewhat tattered feather train. She halted, her mouth open. "There *are* peacocks!" she exclaimed involuntarily, feeling a little thrill of surprise and delight.

"Only Dudley there," said Dr. Moore, glancing back over her shoulder. "He's the last of the flock, poor fellow." She opened the front door. "He and I are two of a kind. I'm the last scion of my clan, now that my poor old uncle Alfred has died. There'll be no more of the Ramsay blood after me, and no one to inherit this mouldy old barn when I go. Uncle Al wanted me to have it—he knew how I loved the place—but it's much too big for me. I don't see how I can possibly keep it up, even with the money he left. I really ought to sell it."

"No, don't do that!" cried Claire in dismay. "It's such a nice place. The developers would ruin it."

"Oh, well, I haven't the heart to sell, not yet. Angus and the cats would be so upset, losing their home as well as their master. I'll stay here a while longer."

With a feeling of unreality, Claire mounted the steps to the wide, pillared front porch. The front door, she noticed, had a brass knocker shaped like a lion's head. Myra Moore went in, followed by the collie, who was now waving his feathery tail in an amiable fashion.

For one brief instant, Claire hesitated on the threshold. Then she stepped inside after them.

CHAPTER 4

THERE WAS A HARDWOOD FLOOR INSIDE, with small Persian rugs spaced along the length of the hall. The ceiling was very high. A grand banistered staircase climbed majestically to the second floor; atop the newel post was another carved lion with a crown on its head, this one of wood. Overhead, a huge chandelier dripped glittering crystals. But it was at the walls that Claire stared most. They were covered in exotic objects: swords and daggers, Chinese fans, and all kinds of carved ceremonial masks—African, Native American, Thai. Otherwise the place was very much as she had always imagined it. There was a table next to the stair—not the claw-footed one she had placed there in her daydreams, but one even more remarkable in appearance: it had no legs but was supported by the carved wooden figure of an eagle, its spread wings holding up the top. It was piled with objects—keys, letters, sunglasses, paperback books, all the comfortable clutter of ownership.

There was a doorway on each side of the hall. One led to a dining room with a vast, dark, polished table—like something out of an English murder mystery. To the right was a large drawing room, with a marble fireplace whose mantel was carved with fancy garlands and flowers. The cathedral ceiling was moulded, with more fruit and flower designs around the central light fixture. The wallpaper was white and green, with a design of ivy leaves, and the carpet was also green, with patterns of pink and gold roses at the corners. Over the fireplace hung a dark oil portrait of a young, fair-haired girl in what looked like Shakespearean-era dress: a blue gown with a vast dome-shaped skirt and enormous puffed sleeves. She held a white cat in her arms, and there were animals roaming through a forest in the background—deer, foxes, pheasants, a huge tawny lion. Claire stopped short, staring at the painting. It looked like an original, but she was sure she had seen it before. Perhaps it had been copied in a book or a pamphlet of some kind?

Myra tossed her sunhat onto the eagle table and led Claire down the hall. Another door on the right led through to a library, its walls lined with bookshelves, its decor all warm earth tones. Fitted into one shelf was a big aquarium in whose depths brightly coloured tropical fish swam; in another was an elegant cabinet containing a TV set and a VCR. There was a model of a sailing ship on another shelf, beside which stood a stuffed baby crocodile and an Egyptian-looking statue of a cat. Claire longed to go into this room, but Dr. Moore had trotted on ahead and she had to follow. There were more masks and daggers on the walls farther down the passage, and one framed photograph. Claire stopped and stared at this. It was a head-and-shoulders shot of a balding, big-eared, elderly man with horn-rimmed glasses, dressed in a tweed jacket and cap. On his shoulder perched a ginger-coloured animal with pointed ears and round amber eyes, which at first glance she took for a cat. But on closer inspection, she saw that it had a face more like a fox's, with a long, narrow muzzle. And instead of forelimbs, it had a pair of leathery black wings like a tiny dragon's neatly furled at its sides.

"What in the world is *that?*" she exclaimed.

"My uncle Alfred," replied Myra cheerfully. "Funny-looking old bloke, wasn't he?"

"I meant what's that on his shoulder?"

"I know, dear, I'm teasing. That's Freddy. He was a special pet of my uncle's, a flying fox."

"Flying fox?" echoed Claire.

"A species of large fruit bat. Uncle Al picked him up on an island somewhere in the Pacific and brought him home. How he got Freddy past customs, I'll never know."

"Your uncle had a pet *bat?*" Claire glanced quickly around the hall, half expecting to see the creature perched like a gargoyle over one of the doors.

"Bats make very good pets, actually. They're social animals, you see; they like to nest together in big colonies. So Freddy was always trying to snuggle up to people. Not that his attentions were welcomed, necessarily. Some people find bats alarming, and flying foxes are exceptionally large. Freddy was more than a foot long, and his wings spanned five feet when they were fully extended. Uncle Al used to greet children at the door on Halloween night with Freddy hanging upside down from one arm. You should have heard them scream!"

"You're using the past tense. Is Freddy the fruit bat no longer with us?"

"No, he died some years ago. But I still have the iguana and the fish and the parrots; they're more than enough! Now, this way to the kitchen." She led Claire on down the main hall and turned to the left.

The kitchen was large, light, and airy, with a butter yellow wallpaper that reflected the sun. It was full of doors. One, in the east wall, led to an old-fashioned pantry lined with shelves, while another, in the west wall, stood open, revealing a ceiling that slanted sharply downward—the underside of the grand staircase in the hall. A flight of wooden steps beneath led down to a cellar. To the right of the cellar door was a sort of square hole in the wall, through which she could see into the dining room; Myra explained that this was for passing dishes through, back in the days when there were servants in the house. "I don't use the dining room much myself. Too big. I have most of my meals here in the kitchen."

There was another door in the north wall, this one leading into the kitchen garden, with a cat door cut into the bottom. Claire noticed a group of small plastic dishes alongside Angus's big metal dog bowl. Cats, too, she thought with a pang of envy. She glanced up at the raftered ceiling and saw a doll-sized figure of a black-cloaked witch hanging from one beam, her little warty face split by a wide grin and her bare feet dangling to either side of her twiggy broomstick.

"That's my Kitchen Witch. A friend sent that to me for a joke when she heard I was interested in the Wiccan movement," Myra said.

Everything here seemed so normal that Claire had forgotten her hostess's unusual hobby. "Uh . . . I hear you got bombarded with teen visitors at your last witch gathering."

"Oh, dear, yes. Most of the girls were after love potions, I recall. Honestly! Wiccans don't do things like that. Even if they could, they wouldn't. It would be very wrong to force anyone to do anything against his will. The Wiccan belief system is all about reaffirming the goodness of the earth, of life, and of our bodies," explained Myra earnestly, "aspects of ourselves that were degraded and downplayed by old patriarchal belief systems. The Earth Goddess movement could even play a role in saving the environment someday."

"I don't understand all this about a goddess. I thought witchcraft was supposed to be Devil worship," said Claire, puzzled.

Dr. Moore looked horrified. "Oh, *no!* If it was, I wouldn't have anything to do with it. Wiccans don't believe in Satan. They worship the earth as a goddess. That's what a modern witch is: someone who loves and reveres nature. In the olden days, theologians and other leaders of society made up silly stories about evil women who cast magic spells and rode through the skies on broomsticks. Wiccans try to dispel that negative old image of women by using the same word in a positive way. For them, a witch is not a sorceress but simply a person who seeks knowledge—rather like the wise women who used to advise medieval villagers on matters of healing and herb-lore, and so on."

"So you're a Wiccan?"

"Me? Well, no, actually. Some good friends of mine are, and I let them use the grounds here for their little gatherings— they like to worship out of doors, you know. But I'm not even an initiate. I just find it rather interesting." She put a kettle on to boil and opened a square, blue cake tin on the counter. "The truth is, I find just about everything interesting."

Taking some muffins out of the tin, she placed them on a plate and brought them to the table. "Cinnamon-apple. They're delicious, if I do say so myself."

The two of them were soon chatting comfortably, almost like old friends. Myra was eager to comfort Claire, and the girl was now regretting the rudeness of her confrontation and felt only too glad to respond. And the muffins *were* very good.

"Were you really mistaken for the Virgin Mary in Guatemala?" Claire asked curiously, sipping her tea.

"Oh, you read about that, did you?" Myra chuckled. "That was back in my young days. I'd always wanted to see the jungle, and I jumped at the chance to go on a research trip to South America. I went on several more jungle trips after that, to places like Africa and New Guinea and Borneo. You see, I used to love the old Tarzan movies when I was a little girl. How I longed to go live in the jungle, and swing on vines and play with the animals! Of course, the jungle's not entirely what it's cracked up to be. You should see one of those liana vines in real life. The wretched things are *crawling* with ants! If you tried to swing on one, you'd get bitten all over."

She poured herself some more tea from the flowered china teapot, looking thoughtful. "But it was fascinating, all the same. Did you know there are pink dolphins that live in the Amazon River? Before I went there, I didn't even know there were dolphins that lived in rivers, let alone that they were *pink!*" She smiled to herself, reliving old memories, then looked at Claire again. "Well, here we sit, the maiden and the crone—two aspects of the goddess, as the Wiccans would say. Take the advice of an old crone, dear, and decide early on what you want to do in life—and *do* it. My Wiccan friends believe in reincarnation, and I hope they're right, because one short lifetime isn't long enough to spend in this wonderful world. But it's still the wisest thing to live your life as if it's the only one you've got. Otherwise you'll decide one day that you want to see the lost city of Machu Picchu, but your arthritic old knees won't be up to the journey—and who knows if you'll get another chance? Seize the day while you're still young and strong. That's what my uncle did. He travelled all over the world when he was in his twenties, and he had some amazing adventures. He spent time with the Bushmen in the Kalahari, and with the Australian Aborigines and some South American Indian tribes, just learning about their cultures and listening to their stories."

"He was an anthropologist?"

"No, he never had any formal training of any kind. He was just interested in a lot of things, fascinated by the world he lived in, and as he'd inherited quite a large fortune, he didn't really have to work but could travel whenever and wherever he pleased. He was my idol, and I always intended to be just like him when I grew up."

"You must miss him a lot."

"Oh, I do. He had a good, long life—longer than most. But I still can't quite believe he's gone." She smiled pensively. "Uncle Al was a special person, the kind you don't meet every day. A real Renaissance man."

"What does that mean?"

"Well, the Renaissance was a time when knowledge was growing at a great pace in all sorts of directions. Many great thinkers of the age—Leonardo da Vinci, for instance—didn't specialize but were interested in several different areas of science and the arts. My uncle was a bit like that. His interests were diversified: folklore and mythology, history, zoology—those are just a few of the things that seemed to intrigue him. Angus MacTavish here, for example"—she pointed to the collie, who was now sleeping on the floor at her feet—"is an offspring of one of his many projects. Uncle Al was trying a new breeding program for collie dogs. You see, breeders are making the dogs' heads narrower and narrower, which makes them look elegant but also makes their brains smaller. The poor things are getting more and more stupid as a result. Uncle Al was trying to breed the brains back into collies."

"Was it a success?"

"Not if Angus is anything to go by," replied Myra ruefully. "He's a sweetie, but he's rather dim."

"I see you've got cats, too." While Claire and Myra were talking, a tabby and a marmalade had come in by the cat door to sniff at their dishes.

"Yes. There are five. Three used to belong to my uncle— Plato, Socrates, and Aristotle, he called them. And then there are my two, Hildegard and Hypatia. That's Hildy there, the grey tabby. It's taking her and Hypatia a while to get used to the size of this place. We lived in quite a small apartment before."

"And there were parrots too, you said." Claire could hear a great deal of whistling and squawking coming from somewhere. Parrots—yet another part of her daydream come to life.

"Yes, would you like to see the aviary? It's in here." Myra got up and led her back into the hall. There was another door at its far end. This led to a second short passage, ending in a glass door. "This used to be the conservatory, back in the old days, and I still keep some plants in here. But it belongs to the birds now."

The air was warm and humid, and it smelled like a cross between a florist's and a pet shop: a moist, mossy aroma of wet soil and vegetation was overlaid by a musty aviary smell of feathers and droppings and seeds. The room had glass walls and a glass ceiling like a greenhouse, and the floor was flagged. In the centre was a concrete fountain with a wide, shallow basin, but it was no longer running. A cherubic little boy held a dolphin-like fish in his arms, a pipe protruding from its curly mouth. Ficus trees and small palms in pots were spaced about the floor, and orchids grew in containers nearby, their creamy or red-purple flowers looking exotic and alien. There were many other plants, too, growing in concrete planters and pots.

"Some of these I brought back as specimens from the rainforests of Africa and South America," said Myra, waving her hand towards them. "Orchids and bromeliads and such. I've got some more seeds and things preserved upstairs. I've been trying to get as many botanical samples as possible on my trips because the rainforests are disappearing—acres and acres being felled even as we speak. Nigeria's lost 90 per cent of its jungles since my uncle went there. Many plants may become extinct altogether—and some of those may have unknown medical properties. Who could have imagined that foxgloves held a treatment for heart disease, for instance, or that yew bark contains a cancer-fighting chemical? What life-saving natural drugs from the rainforest have we lost already, lost forever?"

Claire nodded, only half-listening to Myra's musings. Her attention was all on the birds. There were several of them perching in the potted trees or sitting on tall wooden perches in the middle of the flagstone floor. At the sight of Myra, they broke into excited squawks and whistles. The largest, a glorious creature with a bright red body and tail and splashes of blue and mustard yellow on its wings, opened its hooked bill and gave a penetrating screech.

Myra smiled. "Hello, my dears, we've got company. Meet the parrots, Claire. Technically speaking, only three are parrots: those two green Amazons in the ficus tree and this grey one on the perch here."

"Yes, I know. That's an African grey parrot," said Claire. "And that's a scarlet macaw," she added, pointing to the red, blue, and yellow bird. "And that one's a sulphur-crested cockatoo." The white bird she indicated raised its yellow crest and stood erect on its perch.

"Hello," it said in a little, tinny voice.

"So you know all about birds? I'm impressed!" exclaimed Myra.

"I love animals." Claire looked enviously at the birds, yearning for them with all her heart.

"So do I. You can imagine what a treat it was for me to visit here when I was a little girl. My uncle had even more pets in those days: rabbits and white mice and ferrets, and a tortoise, and a monkey, and a whole flock of peacocks roaming the lawns. It was a proper zoo, and I adored it." She stroked the grey parrot, and it leaned against her hand. "There were two African greys back then: Tillie here and a male bird called Ben, who used to ride around on Uncle's shoulder. Uncle brought him back from Nigeria in the 1930s. Ben died only a few months ago, around the same time as my uncle did. Imagine, that bird was about a hundred years old!"

"Yes, I've heard they're very long-lived."

"Tillie's about the same age as I am, sixty-two. But she's sharp as a tack still. Did you know that parrots are making the experts rethink bird intelligence? It used to be thought that they just mimicked sounds. Now we've found that they not only repeat human words but use them appropriately. One of the cats got into the aviary one day and attacked

Tillie, and as she flew to safety, she called out a whole stream of shockingly vile insults at the cat! Now, my uncle was known to use some rather salty language at times, but how did Tillie know to use just the bad words on the cat? She also has a sense of humour. She loves to imitate the microwave bell, and the phone too. And when she sees me run for the phone or the kitchen, she cackles with glee!"

Myra pointed to the cockatoo. "That's Koko. The Amazons are Polly and Wally, and the macaw is Mac, of course. I wouldn't try to pet him, dear, he nips. But the others are quite friendly."

"Hello," repeated Koko, as if in confirmation. The African grey added a cordial "How d'ye do."

"You're so lucky," said Claire, stroking the cockatoo's soft white plumage. Koko crooned with delight. "What wonderful pets! My mom's cat died a few years ago, and I still miss him."

"I wish my housekeeper liked animals. She doesn't mind Angus, but she can't bear cats and she's terrified of the parrots and Ignatius."

"Ignatius?"

"The iguana. He lives in a terrarium upstairs. She won't even go into that room, so I have to dust it myself. I'd try to get another housekeeper, but Mrs. Hodge has been coming here for decades, and I can't bring myself to fire her."

"Bye-bye," Tillie called after them as they turned to leave.

"There, you see?" exclaimed Myra. "Sharp as a tack!"

They walked back down the hall. Claire glanced into the door of the drawing room again as they passed it. "Who is that girl in the painting?" she asked, pausing. "Is she an ancestor?"

"That's Alice Ramsay, daughter of the laird Malcolm Ramsay. She was a blood relation, though not a direct ancestor. My great-grandfather brought that portrait with him when he emigrated from Scotland, along with those stone lions on the gateposts."

"I thought they looked old."

"They are, much older than the house. They're from the Glenlyon estate, where my ancestors lived hundreds of years ago." She gazed pensively at the portrait. "Alice Ramsay lived there, way back in the early seventeenth century. She was tried for witchcraft, poor thing. That was the height of the witch hunts. She's mentioned in some books on the subject because she was wealthy, which was unusual. Most accused witches were poor women, simple peasants who couldn't defend themselves against their accusers. The same thing goes on today in some parts of the world—certain areas of Africa, for instance. If a person dies of some illness or other, the next thing you know, the whole tribe is accusing someone else of having killed the victim by sorcery. Witch hunts are caused by ignorance, by a lack of education."

"So none of the people who died back then were really Wiccans?" Claire inquired.

"Oh, no," Myra shook her head. "Wicca isn't an ancient religion. It has no connection to the witch trials at all. Wicca was started in my lifetime, back in the 1950s. Its founders believed that there was once an ancient civilization in Europe that worshipped a pair of nature deities, an antlered God and an Earth Goddess. They also believed that the people killed in the witch hunts were the last practitioners of this old pagan religion. The first Wiccans saw their spiritual movement as a revival of a prehistoric faith. They were mistaken, as it turns out."

"They were?"

"Ancient European cultures were polytheistic. They worshipped lots of different gods and nature spirits, not a single god and goddess. Not that any of that matters, really," said Myra. "Wicca's a *modern* belief system based on very modern concerns like environmentalism and equality of the sexes. For instance, when it was first begun, the antlered God was considered more important. But when large numbers of women joined the movement back in the Sixties, the Goddess began to be emphasized much more than the God. Wicca became a vehicle for feminist spirituality."

Claire was more interested in studying the portrait. "That painting looks awfully familiar somehow. Has it ever been copied in a book or something?"

"I wouldn't know, dear. It's possible my uncle gave permission for it to be reproduced." She sighed. "Poor Alice! She hadn't much of a life. Her mother died when she was born and her father was furious because he had hoped for a son. His branch of the Ramsays had become obsessed with genealogy: they were the sort of people who like to trace their ancestry all the way back to some aristocratic amoeba. One of their ancestors was a MacGregor, and the members of the MacGregor clan had always believed that they had a right to the Scottish throne. That's why their clan symbol is a lion wearing a crown. Anyway, this Laird Ramsay's dream was that his son and heir would one day become king. You can imagine Ramsay's disappointment when his wife, the Lady Anne, bore a daughter and died!"

Claire snorted at that. "Inconsiderate of her. Anyway, his own chromosomes determined the kid's sex!"

"They didn't know about chromosomes then, dear. And only male heirs could carry on the family name. He remarried a few years after his first wife's death and eventually got the son he wanted. It's said that Alice always knew she wasn't loved. I guess that's why her family didn't support her when she was accused of witchcraft."

"It's so unfair." Claire felt a wave of fierce, unreasonable anger against this long-dead man. "I mean, what a *pig* her father was!"

"Yes, quite," said Myra, looking a bit startled. Then she adopted a lighter tone. "Ironic, isn't it? All his dreams of a royal line, and the final culmination of old Malcolm Ramsay's heirs and aspirations is—me! It'll all end with me, since I've no children. I don't think the old laird would have been pleased!" She looked at the portrait again. "You know, if Alice really *was* a witch, then I'd be carrying on a family tradition by becoming one, wouldn't I?"

"Is that white cat supposed to be her familiar?" Claire asked. She could not tear her eyes from the picture: for some reason, it fascinated her. The pretty, smiling face of the girl and the blond hair flowing down the stiff bodice of her blue gown made her look very innocent and un-witchlike. *I'm sure I've seen this picture before,* she thought again. *It's not just déjà-vu. But where was it?*

"I really couldn't say," said Myra, peering at it vaguely. "She was supposed to have had a witch's familiar in the shape of a cat. Her accusers said it talked to her and taught her black magic. I don't know if that's the one, though. It might just be a symbol. I believe it was the fashion at one time to paint young ladies holding white animals—lambs, say, or ermines—to symbolize their purity."

"So do you think you will become a Wiccan?" Claire asked as they turned back towards the door.

The older woman smiled and shrugged. "Oh, I don't know. At the moment, I just find it rather intriguing."

"I'm still not sure what it's all about. Is it really just nature worship? Or do they actually believe in magic?"

"It depends on how you define the word 'magic.' Wiccans believe in a sort of life force, a divine energy that fills the earth and all its creatures. Would you like to borrow some books, perhaps?" Myra asked. "I have a couple of interesting ones that might help you understand what it's all about."

Claire quickly said that she would love to borrow them. If she borrowed books from Myra, after all, she would have to return them—and that would mean another visit to this place. *To my dream house,* she thought again. Perhaps she'd get to see more of it; perhaps Myra would even show her the upstairs rooms and the turret with the stained-glass window . . . She went back to the study with Myra, who picked out two titles from the crowded shelves. Then, placing them in her backpack, Claire thanked the woman and made her goodbyes.

Her unhappiness had dissolved. As she rode home on her bike, Claire no longer dwelled on her mother. She could think only of the wonderful house and its amazing collection of animals, and the fact that she would soon be able to return to it.

CHAPTER 5

CLAIRE DECIDED SHE HAD BETTER READ the books when she got home, just in case Dr. Moore asked her about them later. Fortunately, they were actually quite interesting. One was about goddess worship through the ages, a sort of encyclopedia of all kinds of ancient goddesses. She read about Artemis, the old Greek goddess of the moon and the hunt, who was the same one the Romans later named Diana; Bast, the Egyptian cat-headed goddess, who supposedly took care of young girls and women in childbirth; Kuan-yin, the Buddhist goddess of compassion; and countless others. The word "Gaia," she learned, was the name of an ancient Greek earth goddess, and her name was tied into the modern ecology movement. "The Gaia hypothesis suggests that we consider the entire planet as an organism in its own right. This would mean that the earth is, in a very literal sense, our mother. . . ."

The book included a set of invented rituals for women to follow to celebrate certain characteristics of each goddess.

There was an Aphrodite ritual ("Burn a pink scented candle surrounded by real or artificial roses, the symbols of passion, for the goddess of love, and meditate on the gift of romantic love") and so on. The Gaia ritual was to be performed out of doors—"preferably in a wild place with many trees, where you can meditate on the beauty of nature." The book concluded by suggesting that all the ancient goddesses be thought of as "aspects of one mystical being, the supreme Goddess." In this way, women could free themselves from the exclusively masculine images of traditional religions and "seek the divine within themselves."

Claire set the book down. She could see how this goddess stuff might have an appeal for some women, but it really had nothing to do with her. Claire's family had never been the churchgoing type, and since Mom joined that West Coast cult, Dad had been vehemently opposed to any form of what he called superstition: not just astrology or tarot cards or magic crystals, but any belief system involving gods or higher beings of any kind. "Fairy tales for little kids," he'd grumble. "You'd think our civilization would have outgrown all of that by now, wouldn't you?" At his insistence, Claire had promised to devote herself purely to facts: science, geography, history, current events. What he would make of books on goddesses and witchcraft Claire could well imagine, and though she did not take their subject matter seriously, she decided to keep the borrowed volumes out of his sight.

She picked up the second book, which was about the olden-days witch trials. This wasn't one of Myra's books, she saw, but had belonged to her uncle. His name, Alfred Ramsay, was written on the flyleaf, and as she flipped through its pages, she noticed that he had scribbled lots of little notes in the margins. Some were very short, such as "Rubbish" or "Get to the point!" Others ran to several sentences. Many lines were underscored, some with a caustic exclamation point in the adjacent margin. A few of the notes were directed at himself: "Check source," for instance. He had underscored one entire paragraph describing a Salem woman who was convicted of witchcraft just because a neighbour claimed to have seen an "apparition" of her when she was really someplace else. At the bottom of the page, he had written, "Hallucination—or nerve induction?" Claire puzzled over this. She could understand why "hallucination" might be appropriate, but what in the world was "nerve induction"?

According to the book, witches were accused of all kinds of things. People had confessed to having dealings with fairies, keeping familiars, riding through the air on broomsticks, and flying with the aid of magic ointments that made their bodies weightless. Most of these so-called confessions had been made under duress, but some experts suggested that the ointments might actually have existed. Plants like belladonna contained chemicals that caused hallucinations, and ointments made with them might have made people think they really were flying through the air.

Claire yawned and turned to the index to look up Myra's famous relative. Yes, here she was: Ramsay, Mistress Alice. There was only one reference, however, and it didn't say very much. After explaining that most of those accused of witchcraft had been poor rural people, the writer went on to add: "One case, that of Alice Ramsay, was an exception, and though records of her trial are sketchy, it is said that she was ultimately exonerated. This young Scotswoman, daughter of Laird Malcolm Ramsay of the town of Lyndsay, was charged with having a familiar in the form of a cat named Leo, who granted her sorcerous powers. It was also said that she spoke to an invisible companion when she was still only a child. It is known that the early life of Alice Ramsay was exceedingly lonely, and most children in such circumstances will invent imaginary companions to keep them company. On such evidence, slight even for a witch hunt, it is unsurprising that she was not convicted." And that was all. Claire felt rather disappointed; she could not have said why, but she had developed a keen interest in the fair-haired young woman in the portrait. At least the poor girl hadn't been burned at the stake.

She turned the page, and a small piece of paper fluttered to the floor. Claire bent to pick it up. It looked like a sheet torn from a small notepad. Myra's uncle had been using it for a bookmark, she supposed. There were a few lines pencilled on it in his large, bold hand. It looked to her like a rough draft for a poem, one of those modern free-verse ones.

the daimons of Plato
entities free of space & time
see through our eyes
hear with our ears
our world is a game they play
our dreams are their reality

The poem was weird, but so was most modern poetry, in Claire's experience. And there was something rather haunting about that last line, even though she had no idea what it meant. It was interesting that Al Ramsay had had a creative side, too. He really must have been a Renaissance man. She wondered idly if he had intended to write any more verses, or if the poem was complete. The lines looked to her as though they had been dashed off rather quickly, as the words came to him. And what was that reference to Plato about? She doubted he was referring to his cat. More likely, he meant the ancient Greek philosopher. And what, exactly, was a "daimon"?

She picked up the fat little pocket dictionary she used for her schoolwork and thumbed through the D's: *dahlia, daily, dainty.* It wasn't there. Some obscure ancient Greek word, most likely. She yawned, shut the dictionary, and tucked the piece of paper with the poem on it back into the witchcraft book. She had to remember to show it to Myra; the old woman would be thrilled, no doubt, to have this little memento of her late uncle.

◆   ◆   ◆

Chelsea One gave Claire quite a friendly look when she arrived in the locker area Monday morning.

"So did you talk to Myra?" she asked.

"Um . . . yeah," Claire replied. "She lent me some books about witches and goddesses and stuff."

"It's neat, isn't it? Wait'll you meet the Starwind Coven. I want to join them someday," Chelsea One remarked.

"Someday? Why not now?"

"They don't take kids. You're not allowed to join a coven till you're eighteen."

Mimi had arrived, meanwhile, and overheard all this. "Forget the granolas, Chel," she said. "I've found a much better group."

"Group? You mean *another* coven?" Claire asked.

"Yeah, but these witches are totally cool. They're younger and they wear these awesome black clothes, and the

spells they do are different. They can do *anything!* Josie
Sloan introduced me to some of them on the weekend."

A large crowd of girls had now gathered at the lockers,
including Donna and her friend and Chelsea Two. Claire
suddenly noticed a girl standing next to Mimi. She was of
medium height and build, with chin-length hair that, from its
dead-black colour, had obviously been dyed; it did not go
with her pinkish, freckled skin. She wore a sleeveless black
top with very tight black jeans, and on her left shoulder was
a small tattoo of a coiling snake.

"You say they can do anything?" Claire inquired scepti-
cally. "Are they curing people of cancer, then, or bringing
peace to the Middle East?"

The black-haired girl stared at Claire. "What's the matter
with you?" she asked bluntly.

"Claire doesn't believe in witchcraft, Josie," Chelsea
One—or Chel—explained.

"Claire? You're Claire Norton, aren't you?" Josie said.
"I've heard about you. Your mom ran off to join some weird
cult, didn't she? I guess that's where your attitude comes
from."

There were people who could sense pain, Claire thought.
Like sharks, which can smell blood and detect the struggles
of an injured animal miles away, these people had an unerr-
ing instinct for the signals of human distress. And like
sharks, they were merciless. Josie's eyes were positively
gleaming with spiteful pleasure.

"She moved to the West Coast," said Claire stiffly.

"Moved, huh?" replied Josie, throwing a significant
glance at the other girls. "She went chasing after some guy,
didn't she? Said she was destined to be with him, instead of
your dad."

"Who's your source for that?" Claire demanded. A wave of hot anger rolled over her.

Josie only gave an enigmatic smile.

"Cut it out, you two," said Chel. "What's this other witches' coven?"

"The Dark Circle," Mimi said. "That's their name for their coven—isn't it cool? They specialize in spells of power."

"Maybe you can help me then, Josie," said Chelsea Two eagerly. "I want to date Dave Nielsen—you know, on the football team? Sometimes he seems, like, interested, and then sometimes he goes with other girls. So is there, you know, a spell I could use? 'Cause I really like him."

"Yeah, I know one for that," said Josie. "You write the guy's name on a piece of paper, and you bury it at midnight along with a lock of your hair and a rose. Then you say, 'Grant me the wish of my heart, so Dave and I will never part.' You say that ten times over the spot where the name and the hair are buried."

"Or you could pull the petals off the rose one by one," put in Claire, "and say, 'He loves me, he loves me n—'"

"Shut up! She didn't ask you, did she?" snapped Josie. "Do the spell, Chelsea, just like I told you, and by next day he'll start to notice you."

"I'll do it," said Chelsea decisively. "I'll get a rose at the florist's after school, and I'll do it tonight."

"Do these spells really work?" Chel asked.

"Oh, yeah. I got real mad at my boyfriend last year, after I dumped him," said Josie. "I burned his photo in the flame of a black candle. He was sick with flu for a week."

"I thought the Wiccans said any evil you do will come back to you threefold," said Chel with a frown.

The other girl shrugged. "Wiccans don't know everything about magic. There are lots of spells and stuff they've never heard of. Besides, it wasn't evil—I was just getting back at him for some things he said. And nothing ever happened to me, so there. I felt bad about it afterwards, though. I don't do ill-wishing any more."

Josie did not look particularly repentant, despite her words. If anything, her facial expression was rather smug. Claire fought a sudden urge to slap the smirk right off her face.

"I don't believe it," she said.

The smirk broadened into a toothy, challenging smile. "You don't believe I can do spells?" Josie demanded, pushing her face close to Claire's.

Claire looked coldly into the pale, green eyes. "I don't believe *you* ever had a boyfriend."

The smile dropped from Josie's face abruptly, as though she had been slapped. Her look of blank shock was quickly replaced by anger, but before she could retort, Claire had turned on her heel and marched off. She was already regretting the exchange. She had lowered herself to the other girl's level, and Josie did not look like the kind to forget or forgive an insult. But it was too late to take the words back.

♦   ♦   ♦

Once she was home, Claire climbed onto her bike and rode over to Myra's estate. She had intended to keep her books for a while yet, but her eagerness to see the estate again had won her over. Besides, she had read a great deal from the two volumes, enough to put on a convincing display of knowledge and get Myra to lend her some more. With any luck, she could draw this out into several visits—and in the process get to know Dr. Moore well enough that the old woman might one day show her the rest of the house.

When she phoned the line was busy, but at least that meant Myra was in.

It was cooler today; autumn was in the air, and the breeze in her face was chilly. The gate was open when she arrived, and she cycled on up to the house. As Claire passed the old stable that had been converted into a garage, she saw Myra's canary yellow Volkswagen Beetle inside. ("I have a fondness for rotund things," Myra had explained to Claire, "from cars to teapots. I suppose it's because I'm somewhat rounded in shape myself.") Good—she was still in, then. Claire parked her bike, mounted the front steps and knocked with the brass lion's-head knocker. At once she heard a frenzied volley of barks, then Myra's voice calming Angus.

Myra opened the door smiling. "Why, hello, Claire!"

"I've brought back your books," Claire said, holding them out stiffly. "Thanks. They were . . . um, really great." She tried to force some enthusiasm into her voice.

"I'm so glad you liked them."

Claire hoped that Myra would offer to lend her some more books. But Myra only took the two volumes from her with a vacant look. Claire felt, with a sinking of her heart, that this would be the end of it: a few polite thank-yous and goodbyes, and then the parting of the ways. No more visits to Willowmere, no more time with the animals. A hard little lump rose in her throat. Then she recalled the poem.

"By the way, what's a daimon?" she asked, pulling the piece of notepaper out of her backpack.

The distant look in Myra's eyes was replaced by alarm. "A *what?*" the little woman exclaimed, her voice rising slightly in pitch.

"A . . . a daimon," Claire stammered. "I found this inside that book. I think it's a poem your uncle was working on."

"A poem, did you say?" Myra looked bewildered now, as well as startled. "I . . . I didn't think my uncle was into poetry. I can't ever recall having seen him read any, let alone write his own."

Claire handed over the paper. "There's something in it about daimons. I was just wondering what they were."

"Oh. Oh, I see." Myra drew a deep breath. "It's nothing. A daimon"—she pronounced it "*dye*-moan"—"was a sort of . . . of mythical being in classical Greek mythology. Uncle Al was awfully interested in myths and legends. Thank you, dear, I shall cherish this." She glanced at the paper, then tucked it in a pocket.

"Well . . . I guess I'll be going, then," Claire said, trying to swallow the hard knot of disappointment in her throat. She started down the steps.

Myra seemed to come back to herself. "Sorry, Claire, I'm in a bit of a tizzy today. My housekeeper, Doris Hodge, is away. She has an old auntie who is subject to frequent bouts of illness—of the purely imaginary variety, I think. She's been claiming that she's dying for the past fifteen years, according to Doris. But of course, she can't just ignore the old woman—she's all the family poor Doris has. And now my publisher wants me to do some special promotions for my book this week—lectures and interviews and things—and I don't know who on earth is going to look after my pets in the evenings when I'm out. Angus will need to be let out for a run, and they all have to be fed their dinner. I had hoped that perhaps one of the neighbours' children could help me out, but I've been on the phone all afternoon and had no luck so far."

Claire was thrilled. "I'll pet-sit for you, Myra! Please, I'd love to."

"Oh, I wouldn't dream of asking you, Claire. I know teenagers are always busy, what with homework and after-school activities and so on."

"No, really, I'd like to. I'm not just saying it to be polite or anything." To have access to this house, to spend time with the animals—she'd pay to do it, never mind being paid!

"Well, if you're sure you wouldn't mind," said Myra slowly. "It would be a great relief to me to have it all settled. And Pam Robertson says you're a wonderfully mature and responsible girl; she's most impressed with you. And maybe you'd like a bit of pocket money. Besides, I think Angus likes you." The collie had moved over to Claire and was now lying at—or rather, on—her feet, gazing up at the girl with a broad, tongue-lolling grin.

Claire smiled, unable to conceal her glee. "Tell me what days you'd like me to come over."

"Oh, dear. Would tomorrow after school be too soon? And the next day? I've two lectures in a row this week."

"Sure! I'll be here."

❖   ❖   ❖

Claire's father was in when she got home, standing and staring out the front picture window.

"What are you looking at?" she asked, setting her backpack down on a chair.

"There's an owl in the maple tree," her father said. "A little one. On the lower branch there, do you see?"

Claire peered out the window. There was a tiny, round shape on the branch, a mere silhouette. "Hey, neat."

"Thought you'd be interested. The wildlife is getting quite varied around here, isn't it? It isn't just squirrels and raccoons any more. I saw a red fox in the ravine the other day."

"The newspaper said it's all the development up north. The animals are running out of places to live, so they're coming down here. They follow the ravine because it's full of trees and seems fairly wild, then next thing they know, they're in the 'burbs. Did you read about the coyotes that have been spotted?"

"Yes. They're killing and eating people's pets now, I see. Got a couple of cats and a small dog not far from here."

Claire had a sudden, sickening recollection of Whiskers's death. Her father seemed to recall it, too, for he fell silent. She hastened to change the subject, telling him about the offer she'd made to Myra. To her relief, he did not oppose her pet-sitting scheme, insisting only that it not take any time away from her homework. When she explained that she could get a lot of work done at Myra's place while waiting for her to return home, he appeared satisfied. He was partly swayed, she thought, by the fact that Myra was a friend of Mrs. Robertson's. He had a great deal of respect for the guidance counsellor.

Claire was careful not to mention Myra's interest in witchcraft. She did, however, bring up the claims Josie Sloan had made to the other girls. "I don't believe in magic myself," she said quickly. "I don't know whether Josie actually believes she made her boyfriend sick, or whether she's just trying to impress the other kids, but either way, her attitude really annoys me. And some of them actually believed her! I mean, isn't this supposed to be the scientific age?"

He nodded. "I think times of rapidly expanding scientific knowledge are frightening to some people, so they seek refuge in superstition. It's like taking a lucky rabbit's foot along when you fly in an airplane: it gives you the illusion of control in a situation where you're actually helpless."

Claire started to head for her room—but then she stopped and took a little detour into the small den where her father kept all the reference books. There was a dictionary there, larger and more comprehensive than her own, and she took it off the shelf and curled up with it in a corner of the sofa. She *had* to know why Myra would be so rattled by her use of the word "daimon"—if that really was what had startled her.

Dahlia, daily . . . here it was, *daimon*. The word *was* Greek: it came from a root meaning "to part, divide, allocate, apportion." A daimon was "1: in Greek mythology, a divine being ranking between gods and mortals." It was also "2: a guardian spirit or destiny; inspiring muse." Nothing alarming there. Myra had to have had another reason for her brief loss of composure, though what it might be, Claire could not imagine. Her eye moved on to the third definition, and there it stopped short.

"3: see DEMON."

CHAPTER 6

THE ROAD WAS LONG and narrow, with tall trees and bushes growing thickly to either side, its rough surface of unpaved earth stained with their ink-dark shadows. Claire could not see where to put her feet as she ran. Once, she stumbled and almost fell, throwing a wild glance over her left shoulder as she did so.

The thing that was pursuing her looked like a large black dog. As it raced through a patch of road where the tree-shadows were not so dense, Claire distinctly saw its sleek, dark shape, the long, muscular body taut with speed, the questing head held low to the ground. Though it was still about twenty metres behind her, she could see its eyes glittering coldly through the dark. Her head whipped back around and she ran harder, her breath coming in deep, tearing gasps. There were no houses anywhere along this road, nothing as far as she could see but tangled verdure shot with shadows. She flung another glance over her shoulder.

Others had joined the first dog; a whole pack of lean, grey, wolfish shapes now loped steadily on her trail, with the black one in the lead. And they were gaining on her.

She ran on, knowing even as she did so that it was useless: she could never hope to outrun her fleet-footed hunters. She could not even cry for help, for there was no one about to hear her. The wolfish creatures began to bay in excitement. They were so close that she could hear their claws striking the road, their excited whines and panting, eager breaths . . .

Then Claire saw the gate.

There were the two stone posts, each topped by a crowned stone lion, several metres ahead on the right-hand side of the road. Willowmere . . . it was the gate to Willowmere. She did not wonder or question how this could be—even thinking, it seemed, would slow her down—but dashed towards the gateposts with all the speed she could muster from her tiring legs. As she swerved from the centre of the road, she saw a human figure—a motionless form swathed in a black hooded cloak or robe. It was standing on the far side of the street, exactly opposite the gateposts, and though she could see no face, she felt from it a wave of palpable menace. There would be no help from that shrouded figure. But she was at the gate now, and it was not locked; she shoved open the great heavy piece of ironwork and began to swing it shut behind her. Through it she saw the cloaked figure, still standing motionless on the opposite side of the road. It stood in deep shadow, so that she could see little of it, and the face was hidden under the drooping hood. She had the impression that it was about her own height. But there was no time to see any more. The dog-like creatures were running at the gate.

Wildly she fumbled in her pocket. Yes, the gate key was there. Her hands shook. For a heart-stopping instant, she could not find the lock in the darkness. Then the key was turning, clicking into place. She sprang back, leaving it still sticking out of the lock, as a dozen lean, feral shapes hurled themselves howling against the gate. Claws scrabbled at the ironwork, teeth snapped, and luminous yellow eyes blazed at her through the bars.

But the gate held and she was safe, surrounded by the estate's protecting barrier of stone and iron. As she stood there, panting in mingled relief and shock, there was a soft sound behind her—a low, mewling cry. She whirled in terror, staring. But the animal sitting on the gravel path before her was small and harmless: the grey-and-white figure of a cat.

"Miaauuww," it said again, rising to all four feet.

Claire held out a trembling hand. "Whiskers?" she choked.

He chirruped at her—his old familiar greeting—then turned and walked away down the dark drive, tail waving. By some trick of the light, his fur seemed to change colour as she watched: the grey parts disappeared, leaving him white all over. It occurred to her, suddenly, that this was not after all the familiar drive that led to Myra's house. There was a large building looming through the dusk, but it was larger than Myra's place and seemed to have tall towers. Turning back once more, she saw that the gate and wall were still there, but the dogs, the street, and the cloaked figure had all vanished. In their place was a view of hills, grey-purple in the first light of dawn, with a valley below through which a glinting river ran. A sweet floral fragrance blew from the hills on the cool early-morning breeze. And with the scent came a sudden poignant yearning, so strong that Claire almost cried out.

And then, with a sudden start, she woke up.

She rose, feeling groggy and irritable, and stretched to ease a lingering stiffness in her muscles. She felt tired, as though she really had been running. She grabbed her terry cloth robe and headed for the shower.

As the hot, steaming water cascaded into her face, she thought back over her dream. Ever since Whiskers's death, she had dreamed at times of her pet—dreamed that he had somehow come back to her, that his death had been some kind of mistake or misunderstanding. She had not dreamed of him in the past couple of years, however, and had assumed that her long period of mourning for the cat was over. As for the rest, that was clearly a stress response, her subconscious reacting to tensions in her daily life.

Claire towelled herself dry and went back to her room to fling on some clothes. Then she headed for the kitchen, where her father was just finishing his breakfast.

"There's some bacon left in the pan," he said, waving towards the stove.

"Thanks, I'll just have cereal," Claire mumbled.

She tipped some cornflakes into a bowl and reached for the milk carton. Her father cleared his throat loudly, and Claire was instantly alert. That little half-conscious habit of his usually preceded an announcement that he knew she would not like.

"My boss phoned," he said, addressing the words to his coffee mug. "He needs me to go to New York for a trade fair. Just for a few days. I'll be leaving this morning."

Claire froze in the act of pouring milk on her cornflakes. "Oh. That's kind of short notice, isn't it?"

"The man who was supposed to go has come down with stomach flu. I can do the demo for them; it's no big deal. And it's only for three days. I'll be back Thursday evening. I'll ring you every night around ten, just to make sure everything's okay. Remember not to answer the door after dark. And go to a neighbour if you have any problems—"

"I know the drill, Dad." Three days—and two nights—alone. Again. Realizing that she had deluged her cereal with milk, she hastily set the carton down. He obviously read her expression, because he attempted to cast a good light on the situation.

"I'm very grateful, Claire, that you can be trusted on your own. There are some kids who'd abuse that trust—use the house to host huge, noisy parties, get in all kinds of trouble with the neighbours."

Claire stared at her cornflakes, which were rapidly turning into a soggy, unappetizing lump. She wished—briefly, fiercely—that she *was* that kind of kid. The kind who had friends. She imagined them driving up to her door, lots of girls and boys carrying coolers and videos and bags of chips. They'd play Dad's stereo with the volume cranked way up, order pizza, watch the videos together till midnight. Maybe some of the girls would sleep over to keep her company, fend off the silence and solitude. And they'd be extra security, too; if anything bad happened—a break-in, a fire—there'd be all these other people around to help her.

Well, there was no use fantasizing about it. She *wasn't* that kind of kid. Even when she'd had Ainsley to hang out with, the two of them had been loners, not mingling much with the rest of their class. And now even Ainsley was gone.

At least, she thought as she headed off to catch the bus, she was going to Myra's place after school. Of course, that would mean coming home much later, to a house that was dark as well as empty. But she could put off the dismal homecoming for an hour or two.

On the bus ride to school, she found herself thinking again of last night's dream. It was not so odd, really, she decided. The familiar gate on the unfamiliar street, leading to an unfamiliar house, was perfectly typical of the way the subconscious confused things. Everything all mixed up and topsy-turvy. It was the hills that stayed with her— those dim, distant, strangely evocative hills. Their purple colour, the flower scent that blew towards her from them— she couldn't recall having dreamt about a *smell* before. And why should they fill her with this keen, inexplicable yearning?

"Heather! Can I borrow your cellphone?" a girl called to her friend at the back of the bus. Claire sat bolt upright. *Heather.* The name gave her a curious feeling, like an echo of the longing she had felt for the purple dream-hills. Heather . . . purple . . . Of course, there was that plant called heather that grew in wild meadows and covered them in the purple hue of its flowers. But she had never seen any heather. It didn't grow here, on this side of the Atlantic, but was found in faraway countries like Scotland.

Suddenly she understood.

That's it! That's where it all came from. Scotland, the white cat, the crowned lions. And that sense of longing, of heartache even—it's because I love Myra's place, and I wish it could be mine.

Claire didn't believe in dream analysis. Dreams were just compilations of unrelated images, selected at random by the subconscious and thrown together without rhyme or reason. Those dogs and the sinister hooded figure, for instance, were pure fantasy. But there could be no denying the meaning behind the other parts of her dream.

When she arrived at school, the first thing she saw was Chelsea Two walking across the parking lot, arm in arm with a tall, sandy-haired boy. The girl's pink-cheeked face positively radiated happiness. The plump girl, Donna, and her friend Linda Kwan stood by the doorway, their eyes wide. "Hey, isn't that Dave Nielsen?" said Linda, pointing.

"Is it?" Claire also turned and stared.

Linda looked at Claire, eyes widening even more behind her thick-lensed glasses. "That spell she did. You don't think—"

"No," retorted Claire, a bit too quickly.

"But she said only yesterday she was going to try it. Now look at them."

"I don't believe in spells."

"How d'you explain that, then?" Donna gestured towards the happy couple.

"It just happened, that's all." But Claire could tell that Donna and Linda were not convinced.

As they watched, Chelsea Two and Dave walked over to a group of friends standing in the paved area in front of the school building that they used for a smoking pit. Mimi and Chel were there, as was Josie Sloan. The latter was wearing a smug look.

"See?" she said triumphantly to the other girls as Claire approached. "I told you guys it'd work."

"What would work?" asked Dave, standing with his arm draped over Chelsea's shoulders.

"Oh, nothing," said Chelsea, her face blushing bright pink.

"Josie's a witch, a real one," declared Chel. "She knows how to make stuff happen."

"Yeah, right." Dave grinned. "And I'm Merlin the magician."

Josie smirked at him, her pale eyes mocking. Then she caught sight of Claire and her expression became openly spiteful. "Here's Miss Know-it-all," she began.

Claire faced her, eyes steady. "Look, Josie," she interrupted, "I shouldn't have said what I did about your boyfriend. It was mean." Josie looked taken aback; an apology was clearly the last thing she had expected. "But I didn't like what you said about my mom, and in future I don't want you to talk about her like that in front of other people. Okay?"

Chel turned to Josie. "That sounds fair," she remarked in her amiable voice. "Make it up, you two."

Josie's mouth twisted in anger; she clearly felt she was being put in the wrong. "I'll say whatever I want," she burst out, "and if you—"

"Ohh!" screamed Chelsea suddenly. "What's that in your pack, Josie? It's *moving*."

A twitching, whiskered nose had thrust itself out of the top of Josie's backpack. The girl relaxed and grinned. "Oh, that's just Herbie." She reached into the pack and drew out a large white rat, holding it in both hands. It gazed at them with red eyes like beads of blood.

"Hey, cool," said Dave, reaching out to pet the rodent. "You always bring him to school with you?"

"Not usually. Just today."

"I didn't know it was show and tell," muttered Claire. But deep inside, she felt a bit less hostile towards Josie. *Anyone who likes animals can't be all bad,* she decided.

Josie held the rat up to Chelsea's face, and the girl recoiled against Dave, who held his arm out protectively.

Josie grinned and held the rat even closer, making the blond girl squeal in fright.

Then again, maybe she can, Claire amended.

Mimi was not interested in the rat, however. "Hey, check it out, you guys," she exclaimed, pointing. "Who's *that?*"

They had not noticed the low-slung black sports car enter the parking lot, and when they turned to look, it was already parked, its wheels skewed at a rakish angle. Leaning against it in an attitude of insouciant possession, arms crossed on his chest, was a young man clad in expensive-looking jeans and a black leather jacket over a white shirt. His hair was dark brown and rather long at the back, and he wore very dark sunglasses that completely masked his eyes. Claire thought she had seen him somewhere before, and the car, too. Then she remembered. It was the young man she'd seen in the grounds of the big new house, the one she called Dracula's Castle. She again felt a sharp spasm of dislike for him.

"Triple G!" yelped Mimi.

"What?" Claire always had trouble following Mimi's bizarre mix of trendy slang and idiosyncratic, made-up expressions.

"God's Gift to Girls!" she squealed, by way of explanation.

Claire groaned. "Mimi, don't! He'll hear you!" He already had heard her; the bored look on his face shifted to one of weary contempt.

Josie put the rat back into her pack and pushed her way forward. "That's Nick van Buren—he's a Dark Circle warlock."

"Warlock?"

"Yeah, a male witch. And he's *my* guy—my new boyfriend." She seemed very jealous, Claire noted, for a girl who could supposedly ensure her boyfriend's loyalty through magic.

Mimi looked disappointed. "Your boyfriend? He doesn't go to school, does he?" The young man did look old for high school—about twenty, Claire guessed.

"Nah! He's a grown man, my boyfriend. He lives with his uncle in a mansion on Lakeside. They're rich. Some kind of family business, but I don't know what."

"His uncle? His mom and dad are dead, then?"

"Yeah. His uncle adopted him years ago. He's gonna inherit the whole thing, business and mansion and all, when the old man goes."

"But why's he here?" asked Chel.

"He's come to see *me*, of course. Hey, Nick!" Josie strolled over to the young man and began to talk with him. Mimi and Chel watched, open-mouthed, in a sort of trance of envy. But Claire noticed that Josie and the youth exchanged no kiss or any other obvious sign of mutual affection. And his shaded eyes were turned in the direction of the other girls, not down towards Josie's face. The latter seemed to notice this; her expression grew hard, and she moved to stand in front of the youth, blocking his view.

Conceited jerk, thought Claire, and then she wondered why she was annoyed by him. He was Josie's problem, after all, not hers. And he couldn't really be blamed for his uncle's ugly, vulgar house: no doubt he had no choice but to live there.

She turned her back on him and headed for the school entrance.

✦   ✦   ✦

Her mood remained irritable all day, right through her classes, lunch, and study period. It reached a climax in late afternoon when she spotted Chelsea standing at the door of the washroom chatting with a crowd of other girls, regaling them with her story and the instructions for the love spell. Claire could stand it no longer. As soon as the others dispersed, she strode up to the blond girl and drew her aside.

Chelsea smiled happily at her. "Oh, Claire. You want to do the spell too? It really does work, you know—"

Claire cut her short. "Chelsea, think about this for a moment. If it's true that a spell made Dave love you, then it isn't really love, is it?"

The girl's large light-blue eyes looked at her in puzzlement. "Yes, it is—I just made it happen."

"But you can't *make* love happen, Chelsea. Someone either feels something for you or he doesn't. A love spell would be like . . . like brainwashing or something. It'd be totally, utterly wrong."

"I don't see why. I just wanna date him, is all. It's not like I was hurting him or anything."

"But what about Dave's freedom?" Claire argued earnestly. "We all have the right to do or not do things as we choose. It would be wrong to take that freedom of choice from somebody else. It'd be slavery. Would you like it if someone did it to you?"

Chelsea ruminated for a moment, brow slightly furrowed, then she flashed a dazzling smile. "You mean, like, if Dave had magicked *me?* That'd be cool. It'd mean he really wanted me."

"But what if it wasn't Dave? What if it was some other guy, someone you didn't like?"

"You mean some geek, like Earl Buckley in chem class?" Chelsea pulled a face. "Yuck!"

It wasn't very charitable, but at least she got the point. "You see what I mean, then?" Claire prompted.

The blue eyes turned back to her, troubled. "You think I should stop dating Dave?"

Claire suppressed a desire to tear at her own hair. "No, no! That's not it at all! The point I'm trying to make is that it would be wrong if it was true. But it *isn't* true. I think Dave really does like you, and by thinking it was all some silly spell, you're cheating yourself. You're giving all the credit to this imaginary magic, when you should be giving it to yourself and feeling good about who you are. You see?"

"I guess so," the other girl said slowly. "I guess maybe it wasn't the spell after all. Dave *did* seem interested in me before. Maybe it did just happen."

This encouraged Claire. But later in the day, as she was preparing to open her locker, she heard her name called out in an angry voice. Claire looked up and found herself staring into Josie's face. The girl was livid with anger, her pale eyes narrowed and glinting dangerously.

"Just what is your problem?" she hissed.

"You, apparently," Claire muttered as she spun the padlock.

"Don't you try to ignore me. Who do you think you are?" Josie advanced another step.

"Is that a rhetorical question?" asked Claire. "Or a philosophical one?"

"You think you're so smart!" spat Josie. "Where do you get off telling people my spells don't work? Are you saying I'm a liar?"

"Josie, for all I know, you believe every word of what you're saying," Claire replied, dialling the last number in the combination. "But I don't happen to agree with it, and it's a free country, right? So you say what you want and I'll say what I want, and we'll let people decide for themselves what they believe. Okay?" She opened the locker and threw in her backpack.

"You'll be sorry for this," said Josie in tones of menace. As she spoke, Herbie the rat poked his little sharp face out of her backpack, beady eyes staring. Claire was suddenly struck by the resemblance.

"Are you telling me my future now or just making a plain old-fashioned threat?" she asked in a bored voice.

"Just watch it, that's all." Josie started to turn away, then she swivelled back to fix Claire with a hard stare and an unpleasant smile.

"Sleep tight, Claire," she said.

Now what in the world did she mean by that?

CHAPTER 7

AT THREE-THIRTY, Claire took the bus home, stopping there only to dump some of the contents of her backpack, turn on a couple of lights so she would not have to come back to a dark house, and then lock the door again. Then she sprang onto her bike and skimmed off down the street, her heart light. Myra had a lecture and video presentation in the city tonight and wouldn't be home until eight, she had said. That meant Claire could stay in her house for several hours, and she intended to. She had brought some homework assignments with her to help fill the time.

She rode up to the gate under the stern stone gaze of the lions, unlocked it with the key Myra had given her, and then, with a pleasant feeling almost of ownership, locked it again behind her. At the door of the house, Angus MacTavish greeted her with a volley of barks that quickly turned to tail-wagging enthusiasm. She rubbed his ears, then let him out to run around the grounds in the golden evening light, tossing his well-chewed ball to him again and again. When he finally collapsed panting on the grass, she went and sat down by the stone rim of the fish pond.

The fountain was not on, to her regret, but the fish gliding to and fro in the green depths were beautiful and very relaxing to watch. The word for them in Japanese was *koi,* Myra had told her. The still surface above them, undisturbed by the fountain, perfectly mirrored the willows' drooping boughs and the sky above. All around her, the grounds stretched, empty and peaceful in the waning light: from here, she could see no house other than Myra's, which towered in the midst of the gardens with its warm red brick walls and fantastical turret. Seagulls hovered over the lakeshore, coasting on the evening breeze; Dudley the peacock strutted by in solitary splendour, uttered a yelping cry on catching sight of her, and then moved on. Angus suddenly got up, came over to her, and laid his head in her lap. Overwhelmed by this compliment, she stroked the velvet-soft fur between his floppy ears and gazed out over the grounds.

But for a few animals, she was alone in the midst of all this magnificence.

At last she rose reluctantly, gently pushing Angus's head aside. He sprang up and ran ahead of her to the house, grinning back at her over his shoulder. She let him in and entered behind him, turning on the hall light and standing still for a moment in the hall. The house was quiet, save for a few sounds of the kind you do not usually notice unless you are alone: the faint rumbling of the furnace, the monotonous drone of the refrigerator in the kitchen. She thought how different it felt to be all by yourself in a house that was not your own. The vast empty building was not frightening, not unwelcoming. But still there was an *alienness* about it, with its rooms full of the paraphernalia of another personality: furnishings, ornaments, belongings all strange and foreign. The masks on the walls of the front hall seemed to stare at her with their carved or painted eyes. There was even, she half fancied, an unfamiliar quality in the silence that lay behind the house sounds. But that only set her to imagining what the house would feel like if it was her own. She would not stand here then like a timid guest; she'd saunter in from the garden (her garden), slam the door casually behind her, kick off her shoes and leave them lying in the hall. And instead of pocketing the house key, she would toss it carelessly onto the hall table, then greet all her pets, which would come purring and panting to welcome her home.

Angus, eager for his dinner, had gone on ahead of her down the hall and into the kitchen. Claire roused herself from her reverie and followed him, and there found that Myra had left a hastily scribbled note on the fridge door:

Claire:

Dog and cat food in top left-hand cupboard.

Pellets for birds on the table, and some grapes in the fridge (for their dessert). Use the old salad tongs to feed grapes to Mac or he'll bite your fingers!

Help yourself to cookies (blue tin), & anything else you can find, if you're hungry.

Many thanks, Myra

P.S. Could you tape "World of Nature" for me (7 p.m.)? There's a fascinating documentary about newts & I just realized I forgot to set the VCR!

Claire grinned as she scooped dog and cat food from various cans and plopped it into the dishes set out on the linoleum floor. Only Myra could find newts fascinating, she thought. Angus promptly buried his long, elegant muzzle in his dish, eating with loud, inelegant grunts of appreciation. Claire found the salad tongs on the counter, then took the dish of fruit from the fridge and carried it, along with the sack of pellets, down the passage to the warm, moist-smelling aviary. The birds screeched with excitement when they saw her—or was it the fruit and feed they were reacting to? She filled up their feed cups, and when they were done with the pellets, she gave them their "dessert." Mac's grapes she held out to him with the tongs, mindful of Myra's warning. But Koko the cockatoo and the Amazons and the African grey took their fruit gently from her palm, and after she had finished feeding them, she managed to coax Koko into perching on her forearm.

"Hey, boy. I sure wish you were mine," she said softly, scratching the cockatoo's crest. "I wish this whole *place* was mine. But I can always pretend, can't I? No law against that."

"Hello," said Koko, gazing up at Claire with one round black eye.

"How d'ye do," added Tillie, not to be outdone, and pinged like a microwave.

There were no instructions on feeding the iguana, to Claire's regret. It would have given her an excuse to go upstairs. She couldn't help wondering how like her imaginings the upper rooms were, and she would have especially loved to see the turret room, with its round walls and stained-glass window. But she couldn't snoop in someone else's house with a good conscience. Maybe she could suggest to Myra that she add the iguana to her feeding duties, and so get access to the second floor the next time she pet-sat.

She went into the library and, after consulting the TV listings, programmed the VCR. She lingered there for a while, studying the bookshelves—Myra had told her she could borrow any books that interested her—before returning to the kitchen. She did a little of her homework sitting at the table, pausing to eat the occasional home-made oatmeal cookie from Myra's blue cake tin. The cats had begun to appear, slipping in through the cat door or materializing from various remote corners of the house. One by one, they came in on silent, padded feet—a tabby, a marmalade, two formal-looking cats with black tuxedos and white shirt fronts, and one smoky tortoiseshell. They regarded her with various expressions—curious, wary, tolerant—before settling down to their own meals. Angus, replete and content, came and lay down at her feet. She felt suddenly content, too, and relaxed—as though this really was her very own home. The purring cats, the dog gazing up with adoring eyes (at the cookies she was eating, though she could easily pretend it was at her), the cozy kitchen, the well-stocked bookshelves in the library waiting to be explored—all these were, after all, hers, if only for a brief time.

Dusk slowly descended outside, and its grey gloom began to fill the unlit rooms of the ground floor. After a while, she got up to turn on a few more lamps. In the living room, she paused before the painting of Alice Ramsay. More than ever, she felt certain that she had seen the portrait before—not just a reproduction in a book, but the framed painting itself. She had a vague, hazy recollection of seeing it hanging on a wall panelled with light brown wood—yes, that was it: a wood-panelled wall with a high raftered ceiling above. There had been a long beam of sunlight falling across the canvas, picking out the features of the girl's face . . . But that was all Claire could remember. Where was that place, that panelled hallway? Some art gallery she had visited with her parents, perhaps, so long ago that the memory had almost completely faded? She stood for a moment, frowning, struggling to retrieve it. All memories from the time before her mother left were incalculably precious to her, and she begrudged the loss of even one. But try as she might, it remained stubbornly elusive.

She gave up and went back to her homework. But she could not feel much interest in it, and the short point-form notes she had scrawled on the ruled paper seemed to swim before her eyes:

> Rome: a city-state
> mythical founders Romulus and Remus
> expanded and conquered other states
> "All Roads Lead to Rome"

And here, again, she was suddenly jogged by déjà-vu. She was absolutely certain that she had seen these scribbled lines before. Or lines very much like them . . .

Then it came to her, as swift and illuminating as a lightning flash. "The daimons of Plato / entities free of space & time . . ." That's what she was thinking of. That funny poem Myra's uncle had written on the scrap of paper in the book. Only it wasn't a poem, she realized now. *Notes! Those were point-form notes, like these ones I've just written. Old Mr. Ramsay wasn't writing poetry—he was jotting down notes to*

*himself, following a train of thought that had come into his
mind while he was reading.*

But what did it all mean? Daimons, entities, and all that
stuff about playing with the world and dreams being
someone else's reality? Try as she might, Claire could make
no sense of it.

✧   ✧   ✧

Myra came back shortly after eight o'clock. The sound of
the key in the lock and the front door opening shattered
Claire's temporary illusion of ownership: at once she was
only the caretaker, here by permission of the real owner.
Angus sprang up from Claire's feet and raced out of the
room to welcome his real mistress, while the cats jumped
down from their various perches and left the room at a more
leisurely pace, tails in air. Claire quickly gathered up her
books and stacked them neatly, then she followed the
animals into the hall.

"Goodness, dear, you're still here? You didn't have to
stay the whole evening!" Myra exclaimed when she saw her.

"I thought Angus might like some company," Claire
replied. "Dogs hate being left alone, don't they? And my
dad's away, so I decided I might as well do my work here."
She started to head for the door.

"But you haven't had any supper, then!" Myra was horrified. "Aren't you starved?"

"I'm fine. I had some cookies."

"Cookies! Stay and have a bite at least. Please, I insist!"
Myra looked so shocked, and Claire herself was so reluctant
to leave, that it was easy to give in. She joined Myra, Angus,
and the cats in the kitchen, where Myra quickly heated some

homemade minestrone on the stove and sliced up a French stick on her breadboard.

"I taped your show for you, Myra. Why are newts fascinating, by the way?" Claire asked.

"Hmm?" said Myra absently, stirring the soup. Claire repeated her question. "Oh. Well, newts and salamanders can completely regenerate their limbs if they are amputated. That's very interesting because they're not primitive creatures like earthworms, but vertebrates like us. So if *they* can regrow their legs—bones and nerves and toes and all—there's really no reason why we shouldn't be able to do the same. And now some scientists believe they've discovered the gene that controls the regeneration process. Imagine the implications for medicine if we could find out exactly how it works! Human amputees wouldn't have to wear plastic prostheses any more: they could just grow back their arms or legs!"

Claire had to admit that *was* pretty fascinating. "You think it's okay for scientists to change human genes, then?" she queried as the soup was brought to the table. It smelled wonderful—not at all like the canned stuff she and her father always ate.

Myra looked thoughtful. "Well, I can't say I hold with eugenics. I don't think humans should be bred so they're all tall and good-looking and athletic, for instance. Look at poor Angus here. Dogs that are overbred end up with all kinds of genetic defects, like narrow craniums and hip dysplasia. You just can't beat good old hybrid vigour, in animals or in humans—even if it does produce specimens that resemble me and Uncle Al." She chuckled.

"Or me," Claire added, spooning up some soup.

"Nonsense, dear, you're hardly in the same category as Al and I! Not that it should be an issue, really. I do feel sorry for you young girls! I mean, here you are, living in the twenty-first century, with rights and freedoms your grand-mothers could only dream of. And what do most teenage girls think about, day in and day out? Their faces, their figures, and how to attract boys!"

"It's hormones," said Claire, shrugging. "The life force."

"It's the incessant bombardment of advertising for cosmetics, hair products, and fashions," corrected Myra indignantly. "And all those silly, glitzy videos by pop star-lets. Nothing's changed since the Middle Ages, really: girls still believe that their whole existence should consist of making themselves attractive to the opposite sex. At least *you* don't buy into it, Claire. You're not chasing after every callow boy you see."

"In my case," said Claire, "the callow boy would proba-bly run for his life."

"Oh, Claire," said Myra, sighing.

"Seriously, though, I just haven't met anyone special. This may sound corny, but I often feel as though I'm . . . waiting for someone. And he hasn't shown up yet." Claire had never mentioned this to anyone but her mother. It was surprising how Myra put her at ease. She found herself talking on as they ate, pouring out to the older woman all that had happened at school that day. Myra was interested.

"This Chelsea girl, would you say she's pretty?" she asked. Claire nodded. "I think you're right. I wouldn't attach too much importance to all that business about the spell. What probably happened is that the act of performing the ritual boosted the girl's self-confidence. She came to school radiant and certain she was loved, and many men are attracted to confident women. What really baffles me is all this about another witches' coven. I don't know of any in this area apart from the Starwind Coven. Wicca may be getting more popular, even more respectable, but organized covens still aren't exactly thick on the ground—at least not in suburban Willowville. And this young dreamboat of Josie's—you say she called him a warlock? That's very odd indeed."

"Why's that?" asked Claire, finishing the last of her soup.

"Well, Wiccans never use that word. Male witches are just called witches, the same as the women. 'Warlock' is a derogatory term: it translates literally as 'oath breaker.'"

"Maybe Josie just used the wrong word."

"Maybe. But what seems most likely to me is that this isn't a proper coven at all; it's just a bunch of teenagers amusing themselves. Look at these crazy spells they're trying! Wicca is supposed to be about connecting to nature and seeking the divine within yourself, not controlling other people. Wiccans always say that good deeds come back to you as positive energy, while bad ones bring only negative energy."

"Well, Josie had better watch out, then," said Claire lightly. "Or maybe I should be worried about her boyfriend. Think *he'll* come down with the flu?" She laughed and told Myra about the ill-wishing spell as they were stacking their dishes in the dishwasher.

"Ill-wishing? She means cursing," said Myra, fascinated. "It's straight out of the Middle Ages."

"Did that happen a lot back then?"

"It's hard to say really, but I'm pretty sure it did. Imagine that you're an elderly peasant woman and someone has done something to antagonize you. It'd be hard for you to find a way to get your own back—poor and weak and powerless as you are. So you'd invent another kind of power: you'd pretend you could cast curses on your enemies. After a while, you might even convince yourself and others that you really *had* such a power. Imagine anyone doing it in this day and age, though! History really does repeat itself. Because people never really change, I suppose. This girl Josie must feel terribly powerless if she wants to cast curses on other people."

Claire smiled. She felt rather foolish, and yet also relieved. In Myra's warm, bright kitchen, warlocks and black magic suddenly seemed absurd. The Kitchen Witch, hanging overhead on her little broomstick, seemed to mock the ideas with her comical grin. Then Claire suddenly remembered Al Ramsay's poem—*no, notes*—and the definition that she had read in the dictionary. "What about demons?" she asked.

Again there was that strange, guarded look on Myra's face. "Oh, Wiccans don't believe in anything of that sort. Demons and devils are medieval."

"But witches' familiars are supposed to be demons, aren't they?" Claire pursued. "That's what it said in your uncle's witchcraft book. Demons in animal form."

"Modern witches don't really believe in familiars either," Myra replied. "Wiccans may keep pets, but that's all they are—pets."

She still seemed uneasy, Claire thought. "That word your uncle used—daimons . . ."

"Oh." Myra fussed about with the dishes in the racks. "They're something else altogether. Daimons are—"

"'Divine beings, ranking between gods and mortals,'" Claire quoted. "'Also a guardian spirit, inspiring genius, or muse.'"

"You've been doing some research, I see." Myra smiled. "Yes, our modern word 'demon' comes from an old Greek word that had a rather different meaning. To the ancient Greeks, a daimon wasn't an evil spirit, just a sort of minor deity: a spirit that guides a mortal through his or her life."

"You mean like a guardian angel?"

"Exactly. Your daimon was your heavenly protector and guide, helping you to follow your destiny. Later on, the word was used in a more symbolic way to describe poetic inspiration and so on. To be 'in touch with your daimon' was to realize your full potential. The modern word 'genius' has the same meaning: it can refer to either a brilliantly gifted person or a spirit—as in 'genie.' You, Claire, strike me as someone who's very much in touch with her genius, her proper destiny," the older woman remarked.

"I want to be a journalist," Claire said. Odd—she'd never said this before, not even to Mom. Yet she suddenly realized that was what she truly wanted.

She glanced at the kitchen clock and rose from the table with reluctance. "I really should go. It's almost nine o'clock."

Myra got up too. "I'll drive you home."

"No, it's okay, really. Anyway, I came on my bike. I couldn't fit it into your car."

"Oh, dear, I suppose not. Phone me when you get home, won't you? Just so I know you got there safely. Angus and I will see you to the gate."

As she set off on her bicycle, Claire felt a warmth within her that did not come only from the hot meal. It was rather pleasant, she thought, to have someone else worrying about her safety. A friend.

She had not used that word for a very long time.

CHAPTER 8

CLAIRE CYCLED SLOWLY UP BIRCH STREET. It was very dark, and all the windows in the houses were unlit. There was no light on her bicycle, and the street lamps didn't seem to be working along this stretch of road: vast pools of shadow spread under the tall trees to either side. She passed Oakland Lane and cycled on, picking up speed. To her right lay the memorial park, which took up one whole block; a gravel path cut across it diagonally, leading through its dense stand of pine trees to Maple Street on the far side.

As she mounted the sidewalk and turned onto the path, she heard a rustle in the bushes to her left. Someone—or something—was moving through them. She had a momentary glimpse of a long, dark body slipping through the thick clump of shrubbery. Claire stopped, peering at the bushes. A stray dog? Or could it be a coyote? The large ravine where Willow Creek ran was close, just on the opposite side of

Birch. Some people said the animals that had been spotted there were too large for coyotes and had to be wild dog–coyote hybrids, or even wolves. She started to cycle faster, her heart pounding. Though some cats and one dog had been killed and eaten, no human had been attacked. *Yet,* Claire told herself.

It was hard to see her way here in the wooded centre of the park. Metres away, the war cenotaph reared up out of the blackness, its grey granite slab pale in the wan light from the cloudy sky and barred black with the shadows of the trees. She pressed on. Suddenly, the bushes shivered again, just a few metres ahead of her and to the left. She braked hastily, but it was not a coyote-dog that emerged from the wood. It was a figure in a black cowled robe.

It stepped right into her path and flung back its black hood so she could see its face.

Josie. It was Josie Sloan.

Claire yelled a warning, but the girl only stood there laughing, blocking the path. What was the matter with her? Claire rode on, swerving to avoid Josie, who did not trouble to get out of the way. But the bike's handles jerked strangely as she passed the girl, and in the next instant it had gone out of control, crashing off the path and into the bushes. Claire leaped clear as the bike flipped onto its side, then she scrambled to her feet. Josie was gone, but her peals of insane laughter still rang in the air.

Then a dark animal shape burst out of the bushes, white fangs flashing, and charged straight at her.

There was no time to grab for the bicycle. Claire ran down the path, panting, hearing the hoarse, rasping breaths of the beast behind her—

And woke up with a violent start, sweating in fright.

She groped for the bedside lamp and switched it on, then sat up, rubbing her eyes at the blinding light. It was all right—just another nightmare, nothing more. She'd felt a little nervous on that long, dark bike ride home, and also uneasy about Josie Sloan and her veiled threats; those feelings had carried over into her dreams. She glanced at the small digital clock on her nightstand. Two a.m. But it was no use trying to get back to sleep. The nastiness of the dream was still with her, like a bitter taste lingering in the mouth. She got up, pulled on her dressing gown, and went downstairs.

She made herself some hot chocolate in the microwave and went to sit and drink it in the den, turning on the TV for company. She would go back to bed when the evil spell of the nightmare had left her, she told herself. But the fear did not subside. She tried to watch the old black-and-white movie playing on the screen before her, but instead she kept seeing Josie's face from the nightmare and hearing her voice from yesterday, saying, "Sleep tight."

Could she have done something to *make* Claire have a bad dream?

No, nonsense! Josie was just on her mind, that was all. You dreamt of the things that bothered you. Or so she thought to herself as she wearily climbed the stairs again at four-thirty.

But she lay awake watching the sky turn light outside her window, and did not sleep again.

◇   ◇   ◇

Claire went through school that day in a sort of haze of exhaustion and nearly fell asleep in the library during her study spare. When the school day ended, she decided to take the bus straight to Myra's, rather than go all the way home and make the tiring bike trip. She would just have to come home to an unlit house, that was all.

There was a short walk from the bus stop to Myra's estate, but the weather was warm and pleasant, and in the fresh air, she felt less tired. Angus greeted her at the door as though she were an old friend, wagging his tail in complete circles like an airplane propeller, though the cats still held aloof. There was another note on the fridge, this one saying that some of Myra's Wiccan friends were coming over for a get-together. Though Myra could not join them tonight, she had offered them the use of the house and grounds. "So no need to stay late, Claire. They'll arrive around 6:30, and they'll be here till I get back!"

Claire was disappointed. She didn't really want to share the house with anyone. She trudged back down the drive, unlocked the gate again, and left it open for the visitors' cars. Then she let Angus out for a game of ball in the dwindling late-afternoon light. At six o'clock, she fed him and the cats, then went into the conservatory and fed the birds. Polly, Wally, and Koko were becoming quite affectionate, and even Mac didn't scream at the sight of her now. Tillie greeted her with a courteous "How d'ye do" and a very good imitation of the telephone ringing.

While she was giving them their seeds and pellets, she heard an outburst of angry barking from Angus at the front of the house. She ran down the passage to the front door, thinking that Myra's Wiccan guests were arriving early, only to find that the dog was merely voicing his disapproval of the hired lawn-care man, who was returning the lawn tractor to the garage. "Talk about the wolf who cried boy," she scolded him. The collie grinned up at her, unrepentant.

When she went back inside with him, she heard a strange sound overhead: a little impish chuckle. She jumped and her skin prickled. Had she imagined it? No, there it was again: a small, tinny, tittering sound, like and yet not like a human laugh. It was coming from straight overhead. She stared up at the hall chandelier. There perched Tillie, the grey parrot, looking down at her with a bright eye. "How d'ye do," Tillie said, and cackled again.

Angus saw her, too, and let out a bark of fury. The parrot barked back.

Claire groaned. "Oh, shoot!" She'd left the aviary in such haste that she'd probably forgotten to make sure the door was properly shut. She ran back to the aviary and saw that the door was, in fact, ajar. A quick glance showed her that the other birds were still on their perches. Thank goodness for that, anyway. She slammed the door shut to prevent any more escapes and hurried back into the hall.

"C'mon, Tillie! Come on down!" she pleaded, holding up her hand. Tillie put her head on one side and considered the suggestion.

"How d'ye do," she said, and whistled.

Claire ran into the kitchen for some fruit to lure the bird down. But when she raced back, a bunch of grapes in one hand, Tillie was gone.

"Oh, no!" Then she saw the parrot on the newel post, perching on the wooden lion's crown.

"Bye-bye." The parrot retreated upstairs, flying from step to step. Claire followed her, holding the grapes out. Unfortunately, Angus decided to help, lunging up the stairs with another furious bark. The parrot flew up to the landing.

"No, Angus. Bad boy! Tillie! Come here, girl." *Please,* she silently added, *don't make a mess*. If Tillie had an accident and ruined a rug or some upholstered furniture, it might strain Claire's friendship with Myra. She had to get the bird downstairs and back into the conservatory. Then no one would ever have to know about this . . .

"Bye-bye." The parrot flapped away from her, along the upstairs hall. There were more masks and daggers and things on the walls up here, Claire noticed. Doors opened off the passageway—some shut, a few ajar. She caught a glimpse of what had to be Myra's bedroom, all soft blues and greens, and a small bathroom decorated in bright, sunny colours. Tillie made for an open door at the far end of the hallway.

Claire went after her. It was the tower room, she realized, for the walls were curved, following the rounded shape of the turret. She could not help gazing around her, almost forgetting the delinquent parrot. There was the stained-glass window, casting its jewel colours on the carpet: red and gold and green. For the first time, she saw that it had a design of a crowned lion's head in a sort of circular frame, with a motto underneath in some strange language—Gaelic, probably—and a pair of Scotch thistles. The room was decorated in warm earth tones, and it had been made into a study— exactly as she had always imagined it. There was a computer with a printer attached, a few bookshelves, and a writing desk. Myra had all sorts of knick-knacks on her desk, including a little jade horse figurine and a large, uncut rose-quartz crystal—not for spirit channelling, Claire gathered, since it was evidently serving the more humble position of paperweight. And there was the iguana in his terrarium, looking like a tiny dinosaur, and some bundles of what looked like dried herbs preserved in jars. The cover of one small jar was open, and it was full of desiccated leaves and flower heads. She looked curiously at these. Of course—they had to be

Myra's botanical specimens, the ones she'd brought back from the tropical rainforests.

Tillie flew down onto the desk. Claire grabbed for the bird, missed, and knocked the glass jar over instead. It did not break, but its dried contents spilled all over the carpet.

"Oh, shoot, shoot, *shoot!*" Claire dropped to her knees and snatched up handfuls of the dried leaves and flowers. They smelled strongly, both pungent and sweet, and some kind of powder from them went up her nose; she sneezed, her eyes watering, as she replaced the jar on the desk. The parrot, perched now on some loose sheets of paper, watched her with interest. *Oh no, not Myra's papers! Please, please, please don't have an accident on—* Claire seized the bird and held her feet fast with one hand. To her relief, Tillie made no objection but only said, "How d'ye do," and proceeded to preen her wing coverts. Claire glanced down at the papers, which had fluttered to the floor. They were undamaged, she was thankful to see. As she picked them up, she noticed that they were in Al Ramsay's handwriting, not Myra's after all. It looked as though he had been writing some kind of memoir.

"And so I elected to remain in the tropical rainforest of Nigeria for some time. The people were friendly, and the chief knew a few words of English from the missionaries. I learned a few words of his native tongue, and with sign language—and by drawing pictures in the moist mud of the riverbank—we were able to understand one another. The women and children held back at first, shy of this strange, pale foreigner with his odd clothing, but after a time they, too, grew curious enough to approach me, finger my clothes, and even try on my hat, with much laughter. We got along exceedingly well.

"One day, the chief told me that I 'had a spirit.' When I asked if he was referring to my soul, he smiled and shook his head. Pointing to a bird that was perching in a nearby tree, he said, 'There is your spirit.' I said I did not understand his meaning. He then explained to me that in his culture, all men have *ukpongs*—guardian spirits, or 'bush souls,' that take animal form. This bird, he declared, was clearly my *ukpong* because it came to the village the same time I did. I was quite enchanted with the idea, though of course I didn't believe a word of it. I later managed to catch the bird—a type of parrot known as the African grey—in order to take it home with me. They are said to be good pets and wonderful mimics. And what fun, I thought, to tell visitors that this was my guardian spirit, brought out of darkest Africa! I named the parrot Ben, and he is with me to this day. . . ."

There was a shout somewhere outside, and the slamming of a car door. Claire jumped guiltily and glanced out a window. An odd assortment of people stood in the driveway: the Wiccans had arrived. She shrank back. If they saw her up here, they might tell Myra she'd been snooping around her study. Their voices drifted up to her, cheerful and happy.

"Merry meet!"

"Merry meet and blessed be! Rowan, it's been ages."

"I brought my organic apricot muffins!"

Angus barked his head off, but when at last Claire went to the front door—having restored Tillie to her proper place in the aviary—he ran out past her and went right up to the Wiccans, wagging his tail and yelping with delight. He obviously knew them well and considered them friends.

One of the men, a lanky, bespectacled individual with a grizzled beard and thinning hair pulled back in a ponytail, saw Claire watching them and grinned at her. He was wearing ordinary-looking blue jeans and a black T-shirt with a timber wolf design on it. "Hi, I'm Gary Saunders—also known as Greywolf. Are you a new member? You look kind of young, if you don't mind my saying so."

"I'm Claire Norton, professional pet-sitter. And I'm just going," she added quickly.

"Oh, right, Myra mentioned you," remarked a tall, bony woman with extremely long red hair. "Nice to meet you. I'm Rowan Moonwand. She's very impressed with you, is Myra— says you're very bright. I bet you'd make a good witch."

Claire searched for something tactful to say. "I . . . don't know. To be perfectly honest, I'm not really much of a joiner."

"Not all witches belong to covens," said Rowan, looking at her thoughtfully. "Some are solitaries, learning the craft on their own from spell books and meditation. I could see you doing that—walking on your wild lone, like Kipling's cat."

"Maybe," Claire hedged.

There was a real party under way now on the lawn. The group's high priestess, it appeared, was an elderly grey-haired woman whom everyone called Silverhawk. Privately, Claire thought she looked more like a mother hen, plump and matronly and comforting. In fact, Claire was suddenly reminded of her own early childhood days as a Brownie. What was it she and the other little girls had called the two women in charge of their troop? Brown Owl and Tawny Owl. They had been plump, smiling women, she remembered, not unlike Silverhawk, though rather younger.

"Nice meeting you," Claire said, on being introduced to the priestess. "Have a good . . . um, *sabbat.*"

"This is an *esbat,* actually," corrected Silverhawk. "Just an informal get-together, not a high festival. We usually hold them on full-moon nights."

"The moon's full tonight?"

"Yes. Unfortunately, the evening's going to turn cloudy, according to the weather reports, so we may not get to see it."

Claire lingered briefly to ask them about the Dark Circle, but they said they knew nothing about it aside from what Myra had told them. "I wouldn't worry about it, love," said Silverhawk. "I think Myra's right: probably just a bunch of kids having fun. We won't let the youngsters join, so they've gone off to do their own thing."

"That guy I saw—the warlock—looked about twenty."

She smiled and shrugged. "Some people look older than they are."

Claire made her goodbyes, strapped on her backpack, and left. The Wiccans were now arranging themselves in a large circle on the lawn. As Claire walked away, she saw them begin to dance around and around, chanting as they spun clockwise and clung to each other's hands. It looked like fun, she admitted. Once again she was reminded of child-hood memories: square dancing in primary school, playing ring-around-the-rosy in kindergarten. If all Wiccans were like this bunch, it was hard to imagine why anyone viewed the movement as a threat. They were as wholesome as apple pie, and about as frightening.

She walked out of the open gate, still looking back over her shoulder. Then her head snapped around at a sudden deep growl. A huge, black, wolf-like animal stood on the sidewalk, confronting her with bared yellow fangs.

Chapter 9

HER NIGHTMARE OF THE NIGHT BEFORE sprang into her mind, and she almost screamed. But even as Claire recoiled, she saw that it was only a dog—a large dog of the German shepherd type, long-muzzled and sharp-eared, with a coat as black as ink. The dog's owner was standing right there by the gate, gazing curiously in at the grounds and the dancing Wiccans. He was a young man, dressed in jeans and a light navy jacket, and there was something vaguely familiar about him. As Claire edged past him, his black dog snarled again, showing even more teeth.

"Hey!" Claire exclaimed, indignant. "Call off the Hound of the Baskervilles!"

"Calm down," the youth said in a bored, superior tone. He was tall and lean of build, with longish dark brown hair and very dark eyes under strong black brows. He had a sullen, brooding look, like a rock star or screen actor posing for a glossy photo. He was attractive in a way, she supposed—if you liked that kind of thing. "He doesn't bite."

"How was I supposed to know that?" Claire retorted. "By the way, there are leash laws around here." The black dog wasn't even wearing a collar, she saw.

"For people who can't control their animals. Rex won't do anything I won't let him do." The young man snapped his fingers, and the dog went to stand at his side. "But I know you, don't I?"

"Do you?" Claire stopped and stared.

"Yes. You're that girl from the high school, the one who's always bothering Josie. She pointed you out to me the other day. So you've joined *that* bunch, have you?" He jerked his thumb disparagingly at the whirling dancers.

Now she recognized him. Nick van Buren. "No, I haven't. And I don't bother Josie. It's *she* who won't leave *me* alone."

"That's not what she says." He was speaking to Claire's back now, as she had marched angrily away.

She turned around. Nick and his dog were walking a few paces behind her. She loved dogs, yet somehow this great black animal made her nervous. Its head was raised, its tall pointed ears pricked and its amber eyes baleful. "Quit following me," she snapped at its owner.

"I'm not following you. I happen to live on this street. And I don't recall seeing your name on it anywhere."

They progressed for some distance in this fashion: Claire walking ahead with a stiff back and quick, angry gait, Josie's boyfriend and his dog always several paces behind. She had to keep resisting the urge to swing around and yell at Nick. Whatever he said, it was obvious he had been spying on the Wiccans. But why?

He spoke again suddenly as they approached the huge, grey turreted house where he lived. Without turning, she could tell that he was now only a few steps behind her. His voice was pitched lower, even though there was no one else in sight. "You don't realize what you're getting involved in, Claire Norton. You don't know what's really going on here. You think magic is just a bunch of fools dancing around to bad poetry or swapping spells on the Internet like recipes? There's a whole reality they know nothing about. There's more to the world, to the universe, than you or they can ever know. Only *we* know: my circle members and I."

Her dislike for him was increasing by the second. She was *not* going to turn and look at him, Claire resolved. "How nice for you," she retorted, gazing fixedly ahead. "So can you tell me the meaning of life? I think we get tested on that next semester." She jerked her thumb at the Dracula's Castle house as they passed it. "Here's where you turn off."

"I'm just trying to warn you." She sensed, suddenly, a deep and very real unhappiness under his hostility. "You're better off in your nice, safe, happy little reality. Stay away from that old woman, that wannabe witch. She's getting too close, and she'll end up dragging you and the others in with her. There'll be no going back then."

Claire was beginning to feel a little uneasy, as well as annoyed, now. She could hear the dog's panting breaths and the click of its nails on the sidewalk. They had passed Dracula's Castle and the housing development, and Nick was still following her. The bus stop was some distance away. She did not want to stand there alone while Josie's nutty boyfriend hung around and hassled her. She decided to turn up the nearest driveway to shake off her pursuers. It led to one of the larger houses, a gabled Victorian-style mansion with a long gravel drive and woods at the back. But it was, she now saw, not an ordinary residence. The drive led to a large paved parking lot in which several vehicles were parked—far too many to belong to a single owner. There was also a large institutional-looking addition built onto the side, with wide-paned windows like a school's. It must be a private school or some kind of conference centre.

Then she saw the statue in the garden: a robed and veiled woman of white stone or plaster. And there was a neatly lettered sign over the main entrance: St. Mary's Convent.

Claire retreated up the drive. *If he really is a warlock,* she thought grimly, *this is one place he won't want to enter.*

"Ah, a nunnery," mocked Nick, stopping to gaze at it with a sardonic expression. The black dog stopped too and sat at his feet, staring after Claire. "How appropriate—and how quaint. A living anachronism, left over from the Middle Ages."

"Oh, I don't know," she shot back. "Anything you don't like must have something going for it."

"Maybe you should consider taking the veil. I can picture you in a habit, with thick wool socks and clunky shoes. You'd make an excellent nun." He sneered, and the black dog showed its teeth again, as though it was sneering too.

"And *you* make celibacy seem like an attractive option." With this parting shot, she walked briskly to the door. There was a bell, but she did not ring it; she simply opened the door and found herself in a modern-looking hallway with beige carpet and track lighting overhead. A nun in a blue-and-grey habit sat at a reception desk nearby. Before Claire could explain her presence, a door opened at the end of the hall and a flood of people came pouring out. They were perfectly ordinary-looking people—men in suits or sweaters, well-dressed women, even a few teens. With them came music and a smell of incense—not sweet, like the Oriental incense in Books & Magic, but heavy and pungent. Behind came two teenage boys and a girl, carrying a tall crucifix and two large processional candles, and a long procession of nuns walking in twos.

One middle-aged nun wore a white robe and a cape-like golden vestment instead of the blue-grey habit: it looked rather odd with her veil. She saw Claire standing by the bulletin board and smiled.

"Hello, dear. Were you waiting for someone?"

"Uh . . . hi," said Claire. She smiled sheepishly. "No, I'm not. And I'm not planning to become a nun or anything, you know. I just ducked in here for a moment because a guy on the street was bugging me."

"Harassing you, you mean?" The nun frowned.

"Well, it wasn't quite that serious," Claire admitted. She glanced back out the window in the door. "He's gone. I can leave now."

"You're sure it's all right?"

"Yes, really. He was just hanging around outside a house I was visiting up the road. Myra Moore's place." Tactfully, she decided not to mention the witches' gathering.

"Oh, yes, I know Myra."

"You do?" said Claire, surprised.

"Yes, indeed. She came and led a workshop here on women's spirituality. Very interesting, indeed; she's an extremely knowledgeable woman. We're a small convent, you know, and we've converted some of our space here to conference rooms. We hold seminars that are open to the public. Do feel free to sign up for any that interest you." She waved one hand at the bulletin board.

"Uh, sure. Well, I'd better get going before it gets dark. Thanks." Claire quickly slipped out the front door and headed for the bus stop and home.

◇   ◇   ◇

When she arrived, Claire turned on all the lights, as it was growing dark. Then she made an instant macaroni dinner and sat and ate it in front of the TV. When she turned the set off, the house seemed unnaturally quiet, so she switched on the kitchen radio. Claire suddenly understood how poor Alice Ramsay had felt. No wonder the lonely young girl had made up an imaginary friend to keep her company. In the days when Mom was still with them and Dad went on one of his business trips, she and Claire would stay up late together. They'd make popcorn in the microwave and watch some old movie on TV while Whiskers curled up on the sofa between them, purring like a tiny engine.

She glanced out the window. Lights were coming on all over the neighbourhood as families sat down to their dinners, and she watched them for a while feeling envious. Presently she noticed a movement high in the maple tree out front. The owl had returned. She could see its silhouetted shape on a high branch, the round head turning from side to side. Apparently, it liked the place and intended to stick around. The thought pleased her for a moment. Then she felt foolish: she must be getting pretty desperate if a wild bird seemed like company.

She left the radio playing in the kitchen and went up to her room to do an online search on her computer. The words "dark" and "circle" were too general to be of any use, and combining them with "Wicca" or "witch" produced nothing. On its own, the keyword "Wicca" opened up an astonishing number of Web sites, from brief histories and descriptions of Wiccan rites to chat rooms for spells and advice on joining. In one of the teen chat rooms, a fifteen-year-old who identified herself only as Marcia asked the other members for a revenge spell to get back at some kids for "bugging her all the time" and was admonished with reminders of the Threefold Rule. "What goes around comes around," she was warned. A poster who called herself Star Lady wanted to know if it really was possible for witches to fly. There was some division of opinion on this. A few chat-room members said cautiously that it might be possible for an experienced witch, but they advised her not to attempt any experiments.

Claire snorted. *What a bunch of hooey,* she thought. *Pity it isn't true, though: think what we'd all save on airfare.* She ploughed doggedly on, from individual Web pages and sites set up by covens to general neo-pagan and Druidic sites and others dedicated to various specific branches within the Wicca movement. The oldest branch of all seemed to be the Gardnerian one, named after the man who first founded Wicca back in the 1950s. But there did not appear to be any orthodox version of the movement, and there were numerous fringe groups. From what she could tell, it seemed to be a sort of melding of the practices of countless belief systems: astrology, tarot, gods and goddesses from ancient Greece, Celtic festivals, and Eastern concepts like reincarnation and karma were just a few of the things listed under Wicca. One site, to her surprise, even offered a ritual for summoning angels. But there was absolutely nothing in any of the sites about the Dark Circle, with members who referred to themselves as warlocks.

Claire decided to try some of the more obvious fringe groups. She logged on to Pia's Pink Faerie Page, which promised information on "Witch Craft and Faerie Magick." The site's owner invited browsers to "Click on the Broom Icon to learn about the Craft, or click on the Faerie Icon to learn about faeries, elves, unicorns, dragons, and other Invisible Beings that surround us."

Claire groaned aloud. "As Charlie Brown would say, 'Good grief!'" she muttered. Funny, though, that witches and fairies were still coupled together in the modern age. . . . She clicked on the broom icon, but as she expected, she did not find what she was looking for. As far as the Web was concerned, the Dark Circle did not exist. She returned to the main page of her search engine, wondering what word combination to try next.

At that moment, the room was plunged into darkness.

The monitor went black and the companionable sound of the radio downstairs was instantly cut off. Claire sat for an instant, petrified. A power outage, she told herself after the first instant of frozen panic. That was all it was. But that it should happen now, of all times, when she was alone in the house . . .

Telling herself not to be ridiculous, Claire leaped up and groped her way through the room, banging her knees on the furniture. The monitor screen had left its glowing yellow imprint on her retina, so she had a large, square blind spot directly in front of her and nothing but darkness in the peripheral areas. Slowly, she felt her way along the hall. She knew there was a flashlight somewhere in Dad's room—in his desk, perhaps, or in his bureau somewhere? She pushed open his door and immediately tripped on something—a slipper, it felt like—he'd left on the floor. She got up with a grunt and began to open drawers and feel around inside them. Nothing in there that felt like a flashlight.

Well, there were always candles. She had a stash of them in her room, left over from the gift baskets her aunt Marge sent her every Christmas. She went back downstairs and felt around in the junk drawer for a box of matches. Glancing out the window, she saw that all the streetlights were out and the whole neighbourhood was dark. Matches in hand, she went and looked out the kitchen window. No lights in that direction either. This was a major outage.

Then she froze. Two dark shapes, hardly visible in the gloom, were moving through the backyard—dog-like, prowling forms. But no dog would be out at this hour, unattended. They must be wandering coyotes—or wolves.

Claire pulled back from the window. *They're just animals, and they can't get in. The house is locked,* she told herself. *They can't get in.*

She took the matches up to her room, where she lit a small scented candle left over from last Christmas's gift basket. Then she started violently. There was a noise coming from downstairs: all her nerves were on edge, otherwise she might not have heard it, so small and soft was it. It sounded as though it was inside the house. She took up her candle and went downstairs. The sound—a faint clicking, mechanical sound, like metal on metal—was coming from the kitchen. She went in and looked around in the candle glow, but she could see nothing out of the ordinary. The sound ceased.

Then, as she stood there, it came again. It was coming from the area of the back door. She drew closer. Two eyes looked back at her from the window in the door.

Claire gasped and recoiled, her candle flame wavering. It was only an animal—but not a skunk or a raccoon. By the size of those two glowing, pale discs of reflected light, she assumed it was one of those coyotes or wolves, or whatever they were. They were still lingering out there, trying to get into the garbage maybe. This one was standing on its hind legs, pawing at the door handle. At least it wasn't a burglar. Animals couldn't get into the house, not with all the doors locked and the windows fastened. . . . The eyes disappeared. She peered out again and thought she saw a lithe, dark shape leap the fence at the back and vanish into the night.

◇   ◇   ◇

By the time her father phoned, Claire had calmed down somewhat. But she was very glad to hear his voice. "Everything's okay," she told him. "There's a power failure at the moment, but I'm hoping it won't go on for too long. Lucky it didn't come at dinnertime. I'm totally lost without the microwave."

"These outages seldom last more than a few minutes," he agreed. "Have you got candles?"

"Yup. By the way, remember those coyotes, or coy-dogs, or wolves—whatever they are? Some of them are hanging around the house."

"Those pests again!"

"Again? Have they been around before?"

"They've woken me up a couple of times in the night, scratching around the back door. Looking for food, probably. They can smell the kitchen from there."

"There was one—it was actually trying the handle on the back door. Moving it, with its paw. I could hear the clicking sound."

"Just curious, I guess. Coyotes are smart but not that smart. Anyway, no animal can get past a locked door. Don't worry about it. I'll be back around six o'clock tomorrow, and maybe we can go out someplace for dinner. Go to Pizza Piazza or something."

"That'd be great!" She tried to keep any telltale tremor out of her voice. To have him back in the house with her again, a sane, stolid, sensible presence . . . "See you then, Dad."

Once he had hung up, she returned to her bedroom and collected all the leftover candles from her aunt Marge's care packages. The scented soaps and body lotion she had long since used up, and she had stashed the candles in her bottom drawer, always meaning to use them someday. She took them all out now and set them up on her dresser and night-stand. They were short, fat candles in various pastel colours; there was a pink one moulded in the shape of a rose and a white one in the form of a smiling cupid. Some came with glass holders; others she set out on plates and some old ashtrays she found in the kitchen. As the little flames rose trembling from their wicks, the scents of cinnamon, bayberry, vanilla, and lavender filled the air.

She lit the cupid one last and sat back. It looked like an angel, with the flame as a little flickering halo. There was something comforting about it. She almost wished she was able to believe in angels. It must be so reassuring to think that you had a guardian angel, a sort of celestial bodyguard to look after you. Of course, she supposed, you'd likely then believe in the other side, too—devils and demons, the Prince of Darkness—which would not be especially comforting.

The candles were a comfort in themselves, anyway. Their warm, quivering light brought back the familiar room and furnishings and drove the fearsome dark into a few small corners. No wonder fire and candles were used in so many ancient rituals, Claire thought. Already she felt safer.

There were no more noises from the back door.

Claire sat up and read by candlelight for a very long time, then she realized that she was just putting off going to sleep. She was annoyed at herself for her cowardice. "This is dumb," she scolded herself at last, putting her fantasy novel down and taking off her glasses. "I'm as bad as those kids on the Web. I do *not* believe in magic, warlocks, and powers of evil. There are no such things as witches—except for the Wicca type, that is, and they're harmless. All they ever do is sing and dance and play around with herbs. And those animals were only coyotes. I am not afraid to go to sleep. I'm *not*."

She got up, blew out the candles, and lay down again. But her body was tense and she couldn't sleep. For a long time, she listened for sounds outside, stiffening now and then at the occasional creaking floorboard. At least the clouds had dispersed. When she saw the full moon shining brilliantly in at her bedroom window, she was reminded that moonlight was really daylight: the sun's rays reflecting off the moon's pale surface as if from a mirror. She thought of the sun shining on the other side of the earth, children playing under it, people walking around doing everyday things. It was a cheering thought, as though the moon gave to her a little part of their day. She thought of all the neighbours in all the houses around her, sleeping in their own beds or perhaps reading by candlelight like people in olden days. She pictured Myra's place, the old Victorian mansion in its stately grounds, lying calm and still under the moon.

Somewhere, an owl—was it the one in the maple tree?—hooted softly, an unexpectedly wild sound in the suburban calm.

She drifted into a semi-conscious state, her tired mind a welter of disconnected thoughts. She thought she saw old Mr. Ramsay standing on the widow's walk atop his roof, the moon shining on his white hair. He was wearing a long, dark overcoat that hung in folds like a robe, and he carried his giant bat on one arm. Throwing the arm out like a falconer, he released the great black creature to flap away over the moonlit treetops. The image faded, was replaced by other vague and hazy images and disconnected thoughts. Slowly these merged and dissolved into sleep.

What it was that woke her, she could not say. But she came to with a sudden start, feeling disoriented. Where was she? Not in her bed or in her familiar room. There was a blurry, silver brilliance all around her. Then her eyes cleared, and she looked around her in amazement.

She was flying.

CHAPTER 10

THE STREET LIGHTS WERE ALL STILL OUT, *the houses dark; no light but the moon's shone throughout the town. There was no roof above her, no tracery of tree branches to obscure her view: there was only the sky up top and the shadowy earth beneath. She was suspended in the air, flying weightlessly as if on silent wings. The moon floated in a netting of pale cloud, and the night around her was luminous. Every detail of the ground below sprang out at her; every leaf and twig and blade of grass stood distinct beside its sharp black shadow.*

She was not in control of her flight—rather, she was being borne along on the wind, banking and gliding, moving in long, leisurely loops over the roofs and treetops. The sensation was so pleasant that she soon surrendered to it and let herself be carried along. It seemed to her that she turned her head to look back over her shoulder; her neck was suppler than usual, her head able to swivel all the way around. And where she expected to see her back and her outstretched right arm, she saw instead barred feathers and a flapping wing. *An owl,* she thought in bewilderment. *I'm not me at all—I'm an owl. But how . . . ?*

It could not be true, yet it was. It was like a dream that had turned real. High over town, she soared on down-soft wings past Lakeside Boulevard, saw the vast moonlit expanse of the lake beyond and, to the west, the unwinking eye of the little concrete lighthouse at the entrance to the harbour. Over Myra Moore's estate she flew—on, on to the great grey house she called Dracula's Castle.

A bonfire was burning in its grounds, down by the shore. Dark figures danced in a ring around it. Their voices rose towards her on the night breeze. They were chanting, but it was not the carefree, celebratory chant of the Wiccan coven. Its sound was low and monotonous and dirge-like; there was no joy in it, and more than a hint of menace. She started to glide towards the ground, wanting to see the black-clad figures more closely. But there was suddenly a shadow in the sky directly ahead of her, a swooping shape like an enormous bird flying at her, and she was forced to swerve aside, seeking refuge among the dark boughs of the trees.

The other bird was an owl too, a huge owl with dark grey plumage and savage yellow eyes. It pursued her in and out of the trees, out over the street, and across the town. She swerved and zigzagged desperately, and yet it was still as though someone else controlled her flight: no effort of her own could save her. She could only trust in the owl's swift body—the body that was and yet was not hers—in its natural instinct to escape its aerial assailant.

They were flying over her neighbourhood now. If she could get to her home, return to her own form, she would be *safe. Down she flew over the moonlit roofs, coming at last to her own small house. The giant grey owl swooped at her and missed, tearing a feather from her back. She beat her wings — or something beat them for her. Down, down to the maple tree she fled, seeking the dark gaping knothole halfway up the trunk where she would be safe. She could see it . . . she was almost there. Then the big owl dived on her again, claws outstretched, as she grasped for the rim of the hole with her own talons and . . .*

She was safe: safe and sheltered within the tree's embracing trunk. Relieved, she rested and soon drifted into sleep again.

✦   ✦   ✦

Hours later, Claire woke up to the insistent beeping of her alarm clock. She sat up in bed rubbing her bleary eyes. She looked around her room, reassuring and ordinary in the daylight. The power had been restored sometime in the night: her bedside lamp was on, its glowing bulb feeble in the streaming sunlight from the window. The stubs of the candles still littered the room, sitting in little pools of wax, and as she looked at them, she felt rather foolish. The cupid candle looked especially pathetic, with its head and wings melted away.

She switched off the lamp, then dressed and loaded up her backpack for school. She checked the back door, but no trace remained of the nighttime invaders except for a few scratches in the paint and a single paw print in a flower bed that might have been left by some neighbour's dog.

When she arrived at school, she saw Mimi and her friends standing apart from the others in the front yard. They had undergone a striking metamorphosis. Their faces were made up with extra-pale foundation, lots of eyeliner, and very dark lipstick, and they were all dressed in black. Mimi had on a pair of black leather pants with a stretchy black lace top and matching jet-coloured jewellery; Chel wore black jeans and a plain black T-shirt with no design or logo; and Chelsea was dressed in an ankle-length skirt of black velvet and a low-necked frilly blouse in the same gloomy hue.

"Who died?" Claire asked as she passed them.

Chelsea giggled, and Chel said cheerfully, "This is our new look. We're Dark Circle witches now. Everyone in the coven dresses like this." She was holding a white rat, Claire saw. Was it Josie's, or had Chel got one of her own?

"Isn't it cool?" Mimi raved, looking down admiringly at her own ensemble. "It's so *edgy,* and black is totally slimming. And it really, really bugs my parents!"

"That's it?" Claire raised her eyebrows. "You just wear black clothes?"

"No, we actually tried some spells last night," Chel volunteered. "At Mimi's house, after our coven meeting. That's why we've got Herbie. Josie lent him to us—she said he's a power animal, full of magic, and having him there makes our spells stronger." She passed the rat to Mimi.

"Power animal? You mean like a familiar?" History really did repeat itself. Wait till Myra heard about *this.* "I thought they didn't have familiars in Wicca."

"Oh, this isn't Wicca," said Mimi. "This group is new and totally different. Josie says Wicca's for tree huggers."

"So who are these other people? What do they do?"

"All kinds of stuff. We haven't learned all of it yet."

Chel remarked, "We had to come up with special coven names. I'm Catseye, and Mimi's calling herself Moon

Shadow. She got it from a song. Chelsea hasn't thought of a name yet."

"All the good ones are taken," said Chelsea, sighing. "Josie says her circle name is Nighthawk. Isn't that great? I wish I'd thought of it. It sounds so scary."

"Um . . . does she realize nighthawks aren't really hawks?" said Claire. "They're actually related to whippoor-wills, and they're insectivores—that is, they eat bugs," she explained as they all looked blank. "If she was going for something predatory-sounding, she should have called herself Owl," she added, remembering her unpleasantly vivid dream of the night before.

"Ooh, I know—I'll be Screech Owl!" exclaimed Chelsea.

Given the girl's frequent bursts of high-pitched laughter, that seemed an appropriate name. Shaking her head, Claire followed them to the doors. Donna and Linda were standing there.

"What d'you think of Mimi and her gang?" Donna asked Claire, her eyes round in her plump face.

Claire shrugged. "They're just being trendy, as usual."

"But they say this witches' coven is different. You don't have to wait till you're eighteen to enter the Dark Circle."

"D'you think they do Devil worship?" asked Linda, gazing in timid fascination as Josie came walking up the drive. She was all in black denim, with a sort of leather bustier under her jacket and a necklace with an inverted pentacle on it.

"So you've finally chosen your name, Screech Owl," Josie said to Chelsea. The blond girl started, and Claire froze in the act of opening the door.

"I don't believe it!" exclaimed Chelsea. She gave a high, nervous giggle and glanced at her friends, who were also staring. "I just, like, came up with that name right now. How'd you know?"

Josie just smiled. Taking her pet rat from Mimi, she stroked him and placed him in her backpack. Claire still stood motionless. Josie had to have overheard . . . but she couldn't have. She hadn't even turned up on school property when Chelsea made her decision. Had someone else overheard and told her? There had been no time for anyone to tell her anything. She had just arrived that very minute.

Josie gazed at Claire with mocking eyes. "You know why I call myself Nighthawk? It's because I hunt by night." She turned and began to walk down the corridor. "Sleep tight," she called out.

"What does she mean?" wondered Linda aloud.

"Claire, are you okay?" asked Donna. "Your face is a funny colour."

✦   ✦   ✦

"So how's everything?" her father asked as they sat over a pizza together.

He had to raise his voice to be heard. It was a typical evening at the Pizza Piazza, with loud rock music blaring from the ceiling speakers, chattering families, crying babies, and teenage waitpersons bustling to and from the kitchen loaded with pizza trays, salad bowls, and baskets of garlic breadsticks. But the pizza was the best in town, thick and crusty with stringy mozzarella and spicy tomato sauce, just as they both liked it, and served with tall, frosted pitchers of root beer.

"You're not eating much," her father observed, reaching for another slice of pizza.

"I'm . . . not very hungry, I guess," Claire murmured. She rubbed her forefinger up and down against the icy glass of her root-beer mug.

"I thought pizza was your favourite food. You're not on a diet, are you? You're not going to whittle yourself down to a handful of bones, like those crazy girls in the newspaper articles?"

She sighed and took a second slice. "No, Dad. I'm not anorexic."

"Anything bothering you?" pursued her father. "How's school going?"

There were dark circles under his eyes, she noticed, and in the restaurant's strong lights, the lines on his face seemed more pronounced. He was obviously tired from the trip, and he would have to go on another one in a few days—apparently his co-worker's stomach problems still hadn't gone away. But despite his fatigue, Dad was still trying very hard to be a conscientious parent. She chose her words with some hesitation.

"Everything's okay, except . . . Well, there are those girls who want to be witches. You remember? I don't really care what they believe, or what they do, but they're starting to bother me." How could she explain the day's events here, in the cheerful noise and bustle of the pizza parlour?

He put down his mug. "How are they bothering you?"

"Oh, it's so stupid. . . . It's just . . ." She hesitated again, then suddenly she blurted it all out, the whole silly, impossible story. In these commonplace surroundings, it seemed even more ridiculous, and as her father listened in silence, Claire heard her own voice become more defensive. "It really was as if Josie knew things she couldn't. Mimi and her friends told me later that she repeated things they'd said to each other the night before—whole chunks of their conversations—and she *wasn't there.*"

"How do you know that?" he asked quietly.

"Well, she could hardly have hidden in the house, Dad! And anyway, they say they phoned her at about eleven o'clock to ask for advice on one of the spells, and she was home all right. She answered the phone."

"Maybe someone else was spying for her."

"How could that be possible? They were inside Mimi's house. How could anyone overhear what they were saying? It's not like they were yelling at the tops of their voices."

"That's not what I meant. The spy could have been one of the girls—maybe Mimi herself."

Claire blinked. She hadn't thought of that. "A mole, you mean? Well, maybe. But there's still the fact that Josie knew what name Chelsea had decided on. And no one could have told her that, not even Mimi—there just wasn't time."

"Then she and Chelsea might well have agreed on the name in advance and arranged for her to announce it. Then Josie could supposedly have learned it by 'magic.' It could have been a ruse to impress the two other girls—or they might all have been in on it and done it to impress *you*."

Claire felt ashamed to look at him. "They're really starting to get to me. I'm having weird dreams. And Josie . . . I think she thinks she's *making* me have them."

"Your dreams are just dreams, that's all. Josie uses the power of suggestion, and your stressed-out subconscious provides the rest. Claire, you know better than this. Parlour tricks like these have been used to catch the gullible for hundreds—thousands—of years. You've been raised to be sceptical—at least I hope I've achieved that. You know that everything has a rational explanation."

Claire nodded, shame-faced, and was suddenly over-whelmed with relief that he was back.

"By the way," he added later, as he paid the bill, "I hear that power outage of yours was caused by a motorist crashing into a utility pole."

So there: it *had* been an accident. There was nothing supernatural about the blackout either. "Was the driver okay?"

"He wasn't seriously hurt, from what I heard. He swerved to avoid hitting a dog and hit the pole instead. At least he thought it was a dog at first; it might have been a coyote or a wolf, he said."

Claire stared at him. "Really?"

"Yes. I wish the wildlife-control people would get their act together and do something about those pests. There's one accident they've caused already."

CHAPTER 11

THE REST OF THAT WEEK was reassuringly quiet and normal. On Saturday Claire and her father relaxed, read the papers, wore their favourite scruffy clothes, and did their usual weekend chores. On Sunday afternoon, Claire cycled over to Myra's estate with a load of borrowed books to be returned. When Myra answered the door, Claire saw another woman standing behind her, a thin, grey-haired figure in a plain navy dress.

"Oh, hello, Claire," said Myra. "You haven't met my housekeeper, Mrs. Hodge, have you? Doris, this is Claire — that nice girl who comes to feed the animals."

The housekeeper had a dour, lugubrious face and a dour, lugubrious voice. "Pleased to meet you, I'm sure," she said mournfully, extending a thin, cold hand.

"Doris will be house-sitting for me for a few days," Myra explained.

"Are you going away?" asked Claire, dismayed.

"Oh, yes, I forgot you didn't know. I've got splendid news!" Myra beamed. "Sales of the book are going extremely well, so the publisher is sending me on a book tour—five cities across the country! I'll be away for a week, starting Monday. I'm so excited! Mrs. Hodge here is going to house-sit for me while I'm gone. It's very good of her to do it." Myra added to Claire in an undertone, taking her aside, "She can't bear the animals, except for Angus, and it is a big, lonely place. But I'm dreadfully worried about Koko. Whenever I go away for a prolonged trip, he starts pulling his feathers out from stress. He's going to do it again this time, and the poor thing will be such a sight. He needs human company, and Doris won't go near him."

Claire offered, "I could come and visit him for a few hours a day."

"Oh, would you, dear? Koko misses the good old days. Uncle Al always had crowds of friends around the place—a regular salon, it was—and of course, Koko and Tillie and the other birds got lots of attention then. He'll still pluck himself at night, but if he at least had a visit during the day . . ."

"Sure. Unless I helped sit the house?" Claire asked, suddenly inspired. "Then Mrs. Hodge wouldn't have to be alone at night either."

"Why, Claire, that's a brilliant idea!" exclaimed Myra. "If you'd be willing to do it, and it wouldn't disrupt your schedule too much, I'd be delighted. I know the animals would love to have you around."

"If it means I'm not alone with the cats and the birds, not to mention that horrible great lizard, that's a mercy," said the housekeeper, looking relieved.

"I'll be happy to do it," said Claire. To stay here—to sleep over in this house, as if it was her own! "I'll ask my dad, but I know he won't mind. He's going away again, on business, and he knows how I hate being alone in the house. It'd be much safer for me to be here with Mrs. Hodge."

"I'd be glad enough of some company," the lady replied. "This house is so isolated, it gives me the shivers sometimes at night."

"There! That's all settled, then," declared Myra. "I know the house and the animals couldn't be in better hands. I'll phone you to check for messages and see that everything's all right. I feel much better about going now." She reached out and hugged Claire, much to the latter's surprise. She felt her own body stiffen, then she relaxed into the little woman's plump, pillowy embrace. "You're a duck to do this for me."

Claire did not say she was really doing it for herself. She was happier than she had been in many months. A week here, a whole week. At the end of it, Willowmere would feel more than ever like home.

✧   ✧   ✧

Her father made no objection to her plans and in fact looked relieved to learn that she could stay with an adult while he was away, instead of alone at home. Claire went to school the following morning in a happy, buoyant mood. Only when she saw Mimi and her entourage in the hallway did she remember her annoyance from the previous week. Mimi was looking at herself in the mirror inside her locker door and uttering shrieks of distress.

"It's, like, right in the middle of my forehead!" she wailed, pointing to a large red pimple above the bridge of her nose.

"Relax, Mimi. The party's not till tomorrow. Maybe there's a spell for this," said Chel.

Claire said, "There is. Even I know that. I saw a spell in a book for getting rid of zits."

"You did? How does it work?" Mimi asked.

"You go out after midnight, dance in a circle around a red candle, turn three times, and then . . ."

"What?"

"You take a cotton swab, pour on some anti-acne cleanser, and rub it on the zit."

"Oh, very funny," Mimi said, sniffling.

"How *is* the witchcraft thing going, Mimi?" asked one of the other girls surrounding her.

Mimi cheered up a little at that. "It's totally cool. You know, Nick van Buren's from South Africa. He says he learned a lot about African tribal magic from the native people there."

"Cool. It sounds much better than Wicca. I don't know why you ever wanted to join those bunny-huggers. So what spells and stuff are you doing?"

"Does Nick's uncle know what he's up to?" Claire interrupted.

Mimi glanced at her. "The old guy? We hardly ever see him. Nick has a whole wing of the house to himself; it's like he has his own bachelor flat. We're doing past lives now," she continued, answering the other girl's question. "They tested our memories last night. First, Nick took out some really old jewellery and stuff to show us. It was a test, to see if any of us remembered owning any of it in a former life. But none of us did. It was pretty cool jewellery, though."

"I don't believe it!" Claire exclaimed. "He stole that idea from the Tibetan Buddhists!"

"From the what?" Mimi asked, looking blank.

"That's how the Dalai Lama's selected. When the old lama dies, the monks go around showing his former possessions to little boys. The kid who claims to recognize the belongings as his own is the reincarnated Dalai Lama, or so it's said." It was typical of this group, Claire thought scornfully, to rip off ideas from other traditions.

"Well, anyway, it didn't work. We were really disappointed, and so was Nick. Next, he made each of us go into a trance, to try to make us remember our former incarnations through hypnosis. And it worked! It was awesome. I used to be a rich lady in a long-ago time. Nick says it was probably the Victorian age. I remembered my carriage and the dresses I wore to parties and everything."

"I was a queen," said Chelsea. "I ruled this tribe of people back in the Bronze Age."

"Of course," snapped Claire. "Everyone's rich or royal in their former lives, right? No one's ever a reincarnated garbage collector or street sweeper or anything like that."

"But we *remembered* it," shot back Mimi. "Are you saying we're lying?"

That was precisely what Claire wanted to say, but she felt too weary and disgusted for an open confrontation. Instead, she shrugged her shoulders. "Ever heard of false memory syndrome? They say anyone can implant fake memories in your head by describing imaginary scenes to you while you're under hypnosis. It's been done in experiments."

"But we were all right there. We would have overheard if Nick tried anything like that," objected Chel.

Okay, so then you're lying, Claire thought and turned her back.

"Look, Claire, if you're so sure you're right, why don't you just come to a circle and see for yourself? Then you'll know it's for real."

Claire looked coldly at the red-haired girl. She had actually found herself rather liking Chel. The girl wasn't terribly bright, but she had always seemed friendly and honest, until now. Claire would never have believed her capable of such barefaced lying. "Thanks, but I've got better things to do with my time," she retorted and walked away.

"Suit yourself. You others can join if you like. And we'll see you at the next circle, Donna," Chel called out as they walked off to class.

Claire turned sharply. "Donna! You're not joining that stupid circle too?"

Donna looked defensive. "It's my weight. I've tried everything, diets, pills—nothing works. If there's even a chance these people can help me, I'm going for it. You'd do the same if you were me. And don't give me all that garbage about how people will learn to love me just as I am! It's all lies, and you know it. I've seen the way everyone looks at me. Oh, not nasty or anything, just sort of pitying. You know—look, it's the fat girl. There goes the fat girl."

I like you, Claire thought suddenly as she looked at Donna's angry face. There was something about the girl's blunt forthrightness that appealed to Claire. But anything she said to her now would sound phoney, she thought. Donna was plainly not in the mood for what she would see as condescension. As Claire watched the other girl shoulder her pack and walk off down the hall, she felt utterly helpless. It was just like Josie and her idiot friends, she thought in annoyance, to offer false hope to someone so clearly desperate.

◆　　　◆　　　◆

Claire went home to pick up her bike and some necessities. Then she locked up again and set off for Myra's house.

It was a warm day for early October, almost summer-like. Myra's gate was already open, and Claire cycled up the winding lane with a light heart. In her backpack, in addition to her usual homework assignments, were her pyjamas and a sponge bag. *I am going to stay here tonight,* she thought happily, gazing at the brick-and-gingerbread façade of the house. To stay here—to sleep and wake up in this place—was a delight she had never dared to hope for.

Myra Moore had not left yet, but the yellow Beetle's back seat was piled with luggage. As she drew closer, Claire caught sight of Myra in a startling orange jacket with a broad-brimmed floppy hat in one hand, standing and staring up at the large willow tree near the shore. Mrs. Hodge was with her. Claire hopped off the bike, put the kickstand down, and went over to join them.

"What are you two looking at?" Claire asked them, staring up at the tree. She could see nothing.

"There's a big owl in the willow," Myra told her. "A great grey owl. He's visited before, but he's only really started hanging about for the past month or so. He was here quite a bit in late summer. I always knew when he arrived because all the other birds would go silent in terror!" She waved her hat at the tree.

Claire peered hard and finally saw the grey, upright shape on an upper branch, half-hidden by the curtain of falling leaves. Small, fierce yellow eyes peered out from beneath feathery brows.

"You know, there's an owl hanging around my neighbourhood too. He often sits in our maple tree out front. But he's much smaller than this guy."

"He's magnificent, isn't he?" said Myra. "But I'm worried about my cats, and Dudley too. Any of them would make a quick meal for this fellow. Don't let them out while he's around, will you?"

"There are coyotes and things prowling too," remarked Claire. "They've been killing cats and small dogs."

"Put a board or something across the cat door. Dudley has his pen: he should be safe there. I'll call wildlife control when I get back." She sighed. "What a faddle! First I mislaid my Tilley hat, now this." She plopped the soft, wide-brimmed hat on her head; it looked odd with the orange anorak. "For the look of the thing, you know," she explained. "Publicity photos and so on. I've a khaki outfit that will go with it—the sort I wear when I'm tramping through jungles."

Claire grinned. "Have fun."

Mrs. Hodge looked gloomier than ever. "Safe journey," she said, in a tone that suggested she expected the exact opposite.

Myra giggled happily, then she bent down to hug Angus goodbye and headed for the car. "It's so good to know you two will be looking after my pets, and looking out for each other too. Thanks so very much! Back in a week!" Claire petted the whining collie as the Beetle trundled down the lane. When it turned the corner and vanished from sight, her spirits soared in unrestrained joy.

At last, at last, she and the housekeeper had Willowmere all to themselves.

Chapter 12

THAT FIRST EVENING WAS VERY QUIET. Mrs. Hodge went upstairs at around eight o'clock to watch her favourite shows on the small television set in Myra's bedroom. Claire settled in the library to do her homework, then browsed her way happily along the bookshelves. Most of the volumes seemed to have belonged to Myra's uncle; a few looked very old, with leather bindings and fancy gilded endpapers. There were books on travel to exotic foreign countries—some so old that they referred to countries that no longer existed—on history, on mythology, on science. Claire picked up a few at random, glancing at chapters that interested her and at the copious notes Mr. Ramsay had made. She was beginning to feel as though she knew the man, just from reading his scribbled comments in his books. She came across the book on the history of the witch hunts that Myra had lent her, and though she had not paid much attention to it before, she now found it unexpectedly intriguing. The chapter on witches' familiars, she noticed for the first time, had more of Mr. Ramsay's notes and jottings than any other chapter. Why had he been so interested in that particular aspect of witch lore?

She sat down in a comfortable chair and reread the chapter. Familiars were not just the traditional black cats of Halloween decorations, it said, but could also be toads, mice, rats, hares, hedgehogs, snakes, crows, dogs, and various other animals. One witch's familiar reportedly came to her in the night in the form of a ferret with fiery eyes and drank her blood like a vampire. Another witch had a spotted cat that granted her wishes. Familiars had magic powers of their own, since they were really not animals at all but demons in disguise: they could change from one kind of animal to another (the spotted cat, for instance, could also be a toad) or even take human form. A witch could also send her familiar on errands—to spy on people, for instance. But this was dangerous for the witch, because if the demon-animal was killed or injured while it was out on its mission, the same thing would happen to her.

For some reason, Uncle Al had underscored this last sentence twice and placed both an exclamation point and an asterisk beside it; a scribbled note at the bottom of the page read, "See *Ritual Magic* by Aubrey Johnson." Claire had noticed that title on one of the other bookshelves. Curious, she went and fetched the aged volume, blew the dust off its cover, and turned to the table of contents. Chapter 1, "Shamanism," had also been heavily underscored. She read the first paragraph, idly wondering what could have got Mr. Ramsay so excited.

"The term 'shamanism' is now widely used for various forms of primitive ritual and magical belief. The word comes to us from Siberia, where the native 'shamans' have performed their sacred rites for untold years. It is believed that these tribal magicians are served by spirits that appear in bird or animal form. By pure coincidence, it seems, similar beliefs are found the world over."

Claire settled into an armchair with the book and read on, absorbed. "Among the Indians of North America, the guardian spirit usually appears as an animal, in a vision quest or other ritual. The Tlingit of the Northwest Coast believe that a medicine man has several spirit helpers known as *yeks* that manifest in bird or animal form. In Australia, the sorcerer's companion has the likeness of a lizard; among the Yoruba of Nigeria, his servants are owls; in New Guinea, snakes or crocodiles. The Cewa tribe has a tale about a magician who had several hyena spirits at his command . . ."

"Still up, are you?" asked Mrs. Hodge, appearing at the door of the library in a blue flannel dressing gown. "What's that you're reading?"

"*Ritual Magic*. It's an old book that belonged to Mr. Ramsay," Claire replied. "It's about witch doctors and their animal spirits. A man in Africa once told Mr. Ramsay about these magic spirit-animals. I guess that's how he first got interested in the subject. There's a story in this book about an African sorcerer who had a bunch of hyena spirits who went on errands for him. According to the story, they all died at the very same time as the man did."

"You don't say? Gives me the creeps, that does."

"Oh, it's not true, of course. It's just a myth. But here's the funny part: there are really similar stories all over the world—even here in North America, where no one from Europe or Africa ever came until just a few centuries ago. Witch doctors and medicine men always seem to have animal spirits, whatever country they're in. And lots of people used to believe that if your animal guide got injured, you'd be hurt too. And if it was killed, you'd die. The exact same thing was said in Europe about witches and their familiars. So how did all these different people end up with the same beliefs?"

"I couldn't say."

Claire held the book out. "I think old Mr. Ramsay was on to something. See how he's underscored this line here and written a note in the margin? This is the title of another book on witchcraft, with a chapter about familiars. And see what he's written at the bottom of the page?"

Mrs. Hodge peered through her bifocals at the page Claire indicated. The word "COINCIDENCE?!" was scribbled on it in huge block letters. "My, he must have been a bit worked up to write that," was her comment. "What does it mean, though?"

"I'm not sure. Was Mr. Ramsay creating some kind of grand unified theory on animal familiars?"

"Goodness knows. He was a very clever man, though he never went to university. Learned everything he needed to know by travelling the world—or so he always said."

"I wonder what his theory was—if he wrote it down anywhere?" Claire mused. "I guess some prehistoric traditions from the other side of the world could have spread here to the Americas during the Stone Age. There was that land bridge that used to lie between Asia and North America. That could explain all these similarities between Old World beliefs and Native American ones. If so, think how ancient they must be!"

"Goodness, you sound just like the old man himself! It's a shame you two never met. You'd have got on like a house afire. Well, I'm locking up the house for the night and going to bed. Turn off all the lights down here when you go, won't you?"

"Oh, I'm going now." Claire put the book back and turned off the lamp on the study table. As she and the housekeeper went into the drawing room to switch off all the lamps there, Claire glanced at Alice's portrait. Again she felt a sharp stab of sympathy for the long-dead girl. Poor Alice—she'd lost her mother too, though in her case it had happened at birth, so she'd had no chance to know her. *But I can't really compare myself to her,* Claire thought. *My mother isn't dead. At least I can hope to see her again someday. Alice never had that hope. I bet her mother would never have let her go on trial for witchcraft without at least being there to support her!*

"Lovely old picture, isn't it?" said Mrs. Hodge, gazing at it gloomily.

"Yes. You know, Alice sort of haunts me. Not her ghost, I mean, but the thought of her life and how sad it must have been."

"Old Mr. Ramsay was fascinated by her, too. Of course, she was the family legend, so he heard her story when he was just a little boy."

"I wish I could learn more about her."

"What did you want to know?" asked the housekeeper.

"Well, what happened to her. That witch book says only that she was found innocent of witchcraft, and nothing more about her life is mentioned after that—whether she married or had children, or anything. All I know is that her pet cat Leo was her only friend. But he turned out to be the reason for all those accusations against her. People said he was her familiar."

"Mr. Ramsay used to say that Alice might really have been a witch of a sort. What they call a white witch—only he had another word for it. A funny one. Sounded like 'shame on us.'"

"'Shame on us'? Not *shamaness?*"

"Ah, that's it!"

Claire was intrigued anew. A shamaness. A woman shaman. *Could* it be that ancient shaman traditions had existed in Britain—and had persisted right up to the 1600s, when Alice Ramsay lived? Her accusers' claims that Alice's cat went on spying errands for her, and that he was not really an animal at all but some kind of spirit, were uncannily similar to the ancient lore of shamans' animal servants. Was this only a coincidence? Or had Alice actually practised a form of shamanism, the remnant of a prehistoric religion?

I'm getting carried away, Claire thought. But she still felt strangely excited by the idea. She stood looking up at Alice in her fanciful forest. The lamplight gave depth to the painting, made her notice details she had not seen before: birds in the trees; vague, dim forms of animals in the distance. The blond girl's expression suddenly seemed not so much sad as wistful and yearning. She needn't have been a shamaness to be accused of witchcraft, of course. In her day, people were arrested for being witches without any justification except their accusers' paranoia. But it was still a fascinating thought. A person practising the customs of an ancient religion might easily have been mistaken for a witch. Had Mr. Ramsay found some evidence that Alice was a shamaness, or had he just been speculating for the fun of it?

Claire turned out the lights and went upstairs to change into her pyjamas. The room she had been given was a small but very comfortable one, with a view of the lake and the south lawn. The big owl, she noticed, was still in the willow tree: a dark, vigilant shape perched on an upper bough.

The bed was soft and warm as she slipped into it. A couple of cats wandered in as she turned out the light; leaping onto the bed, they curled up at her feet, purring. Claire sighed in contentment. She lay and thought about Alice, picturing the old portrait in her mind, since there was no other image of her. The figure of the blue-gowned girl seemed to be stamped on her memory—and the cat in her arms, and the animals gathered about her in the dim wood beyond. . . . There was something else, though, a poem or song that kept entering her drowsy thoughts. What was it? She could not seem to nail it down. But it had something to do with the picture; more, it was a clue that would explain the whole mystery of Alice—what she really had done and been and what had become of her.

Suddenly, as she fumbled sleepily for the elusive words, they came to her:

Double, double, toil and trouble;
Fire, burn; and cauldron, bubble.

Her somnolent mind could not quite grasp their import. They were familiar words, and if she had been fully awake, she would likely have remembered them. It was something about witches, that was it . . . witches and Alice Ramsay.

Fillet of a fenny snake,
In the cauldron boil and bake;
Eye of newt, and toe of frog,
Wool of bat, and tongue of dog,

Someone was chanting the words, a low, monotonous sound . . . more than one person. Three, she thought. Then, of course! It's the witches in *Macbeth* . . .

Before her the portrait glowed, its colours brighter than before—greens and blues and tawny golds almost luminous and jewel-like—and the gilt frame too shone in the warm lamplight. She could clearly see the flying birds and the animals in the far depths of the forest. The portrait hung on the oak-panelled wall of the great hall, along with all the other paintings of the Ramsay family and its illustrious ancestors. Why she should look at it as if she had never seen it before, she could not say. She had posed for it only last year. How hard it had been to keep still for the portrait painter, and Leo had been restless too—though when she explained to him why he had to keep still, the cat had subsided into her arms.

The three witches droned on, and she shifted her gaze back to them:

Adder's fork, and blind-worm's sting,
Lizard's leg, and howlet's wing—
For a charm of powerful trouble,
Like a hell-broth boil and bubble.

The great banquet hall was built in the medieval style, with a raised dais at one end for the high table, which made a perfect stage. For this performance, the lower tables had all been pushed to the walls and the chairs arranged facing forward. The play was a very good one, Master Shakespeare's latest work, and the troupe of travelling players gave it all their energy. The three men playing the witches wore ragged black gowns and wigs of wild grey horsehair, and they cackled in shrill voices as they danced about their cauldron pretending to throw things in its gaping mouth. Really, they were almost more funny than frightening.

Her attention wandered again. Father sat two chairs away, in his very best lace ruff and black velvet doublet with matching trunk hose. Next to him, her stepmother looked small and mousy despite her fine garnet-coloured gown, which had been made to the latest fashion, with its drum-shaped farthingale skirt and huge neck ruff. Lady Euphemia's thin, fawn-coloured hair was escaping in straggling strands from its piled coiffure, and her pale, pinched face was downcast. It was said she was with child again and likely dreading the birth, fearing she would bear yet another daughter and incur Father's wrath. The poor woman.

She looked down at her own deep-blue gown, with its tight-buttoned bodice and wide peplum and huge hooped skirts. Her tall whisk collar, supported on its wire frame, was scratchy and confining, and her hair was pulled tightly over a pad on the crown of her head, making her head ache. She longed to wear it down, as she had been allowed to do when she was younger. On her breast lay the golden chain from which hung the great teardrop-shaped pearl: her father's bridal gift to her late mother. All her father's gifts were regal and extravagant, gifts fit for a king.

Nurse didn't like the necklace and sighed whenever she put it around her young charge's neck. "Unlucky, that pearl," she said. "It will bring nothing but tears. It brought sorrow to your poor mother, and it will do the same for you if you wear it."

Whenever she wore it, she always thought of her mother. She wondered if she had been happy with Father, or if she *had looked as miserable as poor Lady Euphemia did now. And would she too sit like that one day by the side of her own husband—too miserable to give heed to anything around her? She knew her father intended her to marry Sir Ian Macfarlane's eldest son. He was a wealthy landowner, after all, and his son Alasdair would one day inherit his property. She could not bear to think of it. Thinking about marriage was like thinking about death or the end of the world—one's thoughts veered away, consigning it to the distant future. But she could not help stealing a glance at the young man sitting at the far end of the row of chairs, with his parents and his young sister, Helen. Alasdair was growing thick-set and lumpish and ruddy-cheeked like his father. His eyes were glazed with boredom, and he fidgeted as he watched the play. How different he was from his cousin! William Macfarlane sat bolt upright, his blue eyes alight with interest, the soft brown fringe of his short beard and his curly nut brown hair glossy in the candlelight. If it was Will . . . She believed she wouldn't mind at all being married to Will. He laughed more, and he had such a lively and intelligent mind. She had missed him terribly when he was away at the university in Paris. She was glad he was back again, though there were rumours that he might be travelling to the New World next. Well, it couldn't be helped. She must try hard not to think about it.*

The play paused now, as the set had to be changed. The audience streamed from the hall, stretching their legs, talking, and gossiping as they waited for the entertainment to recommence.

As she walked out with the others, she found William Macfarlane at her elbow, smiling down at her with his clear blue eyes. "What think you of the play, Princess Alice?" He always called her by this title, in a playful manner.

She returned his smile. "I like it well: I am very fond of all Master Shakespeare's works. I only wish I could have seen it performed in London. The theatres there must be quite magnificent. Did you enjoy your time in Paris, Will?"

He gave a little grimace. "I saw little enough of the city; a scholar must keep his nose in his books. But we learnt many wonderful things. I feel I am a better man for having read Virgil and the Greek philosophers and the theories of Copernicus—"

"Oh, Copernicus! It is so hard to believe what he said, that the earth moves about the sun and not the other way around."

"Spin around, my princess. Now, does that candle on the wall bracket not seem to move as you turn? And to vanish when your back is towards it? Yet it is standing still; it is you who are moving. So it is with the sun and the earth."

"How wonderful. I wish I could go to the university too. I would dearly love to see Paris!"

"There! You believe in Paris, do you not, even though you cannot see it?"

She laughed. She still felt a little dizzy from spinning around, and her next words came out before she thought. "Oh, I believe in things that cannot be seen! There is my angel, for instance."

He smiled. "Your guardian angel, you mean?"

"Aye, so he must be. He has always been with me, ever since I can remember. He has warned me away from dangers and comforted me when I was lonely. Life would be a terrible thing without my good angel to bear me company!"

Now he was frowning. "He speaks to you, you mean?"

"Not in words, as you are speaking now. But I know he is there. I . . . feel him." She looked up into his face. This was

Will: he was her dear friend, and soon he might be leaving her forever. "Will, it may be hard for you to believe, but he truly is real. He even has a name. I call him Leo, because when I was very little, I used to imagine that he looked like the lion on our family crest."

"Leo?" William glanced at the white cat curled up on a nearby windowsill. "Now you are teasing me, are you not? Leo is the name of your cat!"

She drew close to him, spoke in a low voice. "He is not just a cat. I asked my guardian one day if he could take a visible form, so that I might see him and touch him. And the very next day, this cat appeared in the forest when I was out walking, and it followed me to my door. I asked my guardian spirit if he and this cat were one and the same, and Leo said it was so."

His face filled with alarm. He looked around him quickly, then pulled her aside and spoke urgently in her ear. "Alice, do not speak of this to anyone! It is a pretty fancy, but a witch finder might misinterpret your words. There are two of them here in the village, did you not know? People have been burnt for saying they keep company with spirits."

"I have told no one but you. Do you believe in witches, Will—like those ones in the play?"

"No, I do not. They are only a superstition."

"The king did not believe in them once, but now he says they are real."

At the start of his reign, King James and his bride had almost been shipwrecked in a great storm, and a group of witches in North Berwick had been tried and executed for summoning the storm by sorcery. It was said that one defiant witch proved her guilt by repeating, word for word, every-thing that was said between the king and his bride on their *wedding night. He had instituted stern laws against witch-craft since and had written a book on the subject, the Daemonologie.*

"His Majesty may believe what he pleases. For my part, I am more afraid of witch hunters than witches. Master Edward Morley and Master Anthony King have killed more than a hundred people already—young girls and women, for the most part." At that, she was silent, appalled. *"I do not believe they will dare to harm you, laird's daughter that you are; it is mainly villagers they kill. And your father enjoys good favour at court. But, Alice, have a care!"* He held out his arm. *"Now let us go back to watch the play and speak no more of this."*

She reached out to place her arm in his—

But in that instant, the great panelled passageway quivered, dimmed, and vanished.

Claire gave a violent start and sat bolt upright in bed, looking wildly about her. She was still in the spare bedroom—in her confusion, it took her a moment to remember why her surroundings were strange—and the house was utterly still. Tree branches tossed in a light wind outside, and the cats purred on at her feet, but there was no other sound. Claire sat for a long time, shaking and perspiring, staring wide-eyed into the dark.

CHAPTER 13

"IT WASN'T A DREAM," Claire insisted.

She had gone straight to the sick room at Willowville High that morning, skipping homeroom to talk to the school nurse. The woman looked kindly and patient but a bit doubtful.

"You say you were in bed."

"I know, but it wasn't a dream. It was too real. It's not the first time this has happened either. The first one I had . . . I know this sounds weird, but in it I felt as if I'd turned into an owl. There was a real owl in a tree at the front of our property. I could hear it hooting as I lay in bed, and then suddenly it was as if I *was* the owl. Flying through the air. And then last night, it was even longer, maybe half an hour or more. I thought I was this girl from a long time ago, someone I'd been thinking about moments before . . ."

"What do you think is causing this?" the nurse asked.

Claire hesitated. "I think it's something I came in contact with at my friend's place," she explained. "It must be. Her house is full of bizarre plants. She's got some strange ones in a sort of greenhouse, and some dried herbs or something in a room upstairs. There were some in this jar that accidentally got knocked over. I scooped the stuff up and put it back, but I breathed some of it in. That same night, I had the first hallucination, when I thought I was flying. I read in a book about an ointment with a herb in it that makes people think they can fly—belladonna or something."

"Oh, you kids and your drugs," said the nurse, sighing.

"I don't do drugs," retorted Claire, indignant. "I'm not an idiot. And Myra doesn't do them either. Look." She pulled the jar of dried plants, wrapped in plastic, out of her backpack and held it out.

The nurse took it, opened the jar, and prodded the contents with her forefinger. "Looks like plain old potpourri to me."

"Like what?"

"Flowers, dried and preserved for their fragrance. Lots of people make potpourri."

Claire shook her head. "You don't understand. Myra's a nature writer. She travels to places like the Amazon, and sometimes she brings plants and things back with her. Some of them may have unknown properties, she says. She's away now, so I can't ask her what this stuff is made of, but I wondered if it could have affected me in some way."

"I don't see how, unless you did something crazy like ate it or smoked it. And probably not even then. It still just looks like ordinary flowers to me. I'm almost sure this one's a rosebud." The nurse put the lid back on the jar and handed it over. "Well, you'll just have to ask her about it when she gets back. In the meantime, see your doctor if it happens again. Are you getting enough sleep at night?"

"Well, not a lot," Claire confessed. "I didn't sleep at all last night—but that was after I had the hallucination."

"How about the night before? Insomnia can cause hallucinations if it goes on long enough. You kids are always burning the candle at both ends—no wonder you end up getting sick."

Claire gave up. As she left the sick room, she passed Mrs. Robertson in the hall.

"Are you not feeling well, Claire?" the counsellor asked, stopping.

Claire was getting tired of talking about the "dream that wasn't." She was even beginning to wonder if it might not have been a dream, after all. "I'm fine," she said in her most off-putting voice and headed down the hall at a brisk pace.

◇   ◇   ◇

In her spare period that afternoon, she went to the library and looked up all the books that contained information on old-time witchcraft. The flying ointment was described in a couple of books, but there was nothing about the herbs it might have contained. Nor was there anything about a potion or ointment that might cause vivid dreams of faraway times or places. Claire decided to follow the nurse's advice and make a doctor's appointment when she got back to Willowmere. She was on the point of reshelving the books when another thought occurred to her. She checked each index again, but it was in vain: apparently, Alice Ramsay did not merit a mention either. She did manage to find a book, *A Guide to Scotland,* that contained a reference to the town of Lyndsay. But it seemed that the town no longer existed. The valley in which it had lain had been deliberately flooded back in the 1970s to form a reservoir. The tenants' cottages, the church, and the ruined shell of the old manor house (which according to the guide had burned to the ground at the turn of the last century) were drowned now in fathoms of water. There would be no church registry to check, then—no records of any kind. So there was no way to determine if Alice had really married someone named Macfarlane.

But of course she hadn't. The idea was silly. The whole thing had been a delusion, a mind-trip like the flying sequence Claire had had before, induced by strange chemicals or fatigue, or possibly a combination of both.

When Claire returned to Myra's estate after school, she saw Nick van Buren standing and peering through the gates again. "Sorry to interrupt your loitering," she said as she walked up behind him. He jumped, looking guilty, then annoyed.

"I was waiting for you," he began.

"Oh, really. Did we have an appointment?" She unlocked the gate.

"You've ignored all my warnings. They're starting to talk about you at the circle, did you know that? You don't know the danger you're in, you little fool. You've got to stay away from this place."

Claire slammed the gate in his face. "Bug off, or I'll call the cops and say you're stalking me."

His handsome face flushed. "Don't flatter yourself." He turned on his heel and strode off while she was trying to come up with a suitable rejoinder.

As she approached the house, Claire noticed that Mrs. Hodge's car wasn't in the garage. She was probably out shopping. All the better—Claire could have the house to herself. She let herself in and was pounced on by a joyous Angus. "Down, boy, down," she murmured happily as he flung himself against her again and again, tail whirling in circles. "Want to go for a run?"

He tore out the door into the yard, running like a greyhound, and she followed at a leisurely pace, hands in her pockets. Dudley yelped at her from his enclosure by the old greenhouse—no doubt he, like the cats, resented not being allowed out. Claire glanced up at the tree. Yes, the grey shape of the owl was still there, waiting patiently on a bough. Fascinating as the big bird was, she wished he would take himself off. He was an intrusion on the peaceful garden and a nuisance.

"Okay, you can stick around for a while," she said to him. "But after that, we're calling wildlife control." The owl ignored her, its keen yellow eyes gazing off into space.

She played ball with Angus for half an hour or so, then took him back inside. When she went into the kitchen, she saw a note on the refrigerator and went over to read it.

Dear Claire:

I've got to make an unexpected trip to Buffalo. My old aunt's very ill, and as she's all the family I have, I really must go to her. I'm sorry to leave you like this. Don't bother with the cleaning, I'll catch up on it when I get back. I shouldn't be more than two or three days.

Mrs. Hodge

Claire stared at the note. So the old lady was having another of her false alarms and Mrs. Hodge was gone—for three days, maybe. Perhaps even longer, if this latest bout of hypochondria was a serious play for sympathy. Claire was all alone in the house. She stood staring at the note on the fridge as this knowledge sank in.

Then slowly, as if in a trance, Claire walked back out into the warm autumn sunlight. The trees were still very green, only a touch of red in one or two of the maples near the edge of the property. She walked to the brook, with its humpbacked Chinese bridges and bronze wading cranes, and came to the pool with the fountain. She went into the nearby summer house with the pagoda roof and flipped the switch that turned the fountain on. The tall plume of spray rose into the sunlit air at once. She gazed at its luminous column for a time, then went back to the summer house and flicked the switch again. The plume quivered and dropped, obedient to her command. A wide grin spread across her face.

Mine. My place. For three days . . . All mine!

Dad had not yet left for his trip, but she wouldn't tell him of this development: he'd insist she come home at once for safety's sake. But it was one thing to be alone at home and another to have Willowmere to herself. *Mine, for a time—all mine.* She knew she was probably being reckless, but in the warm sunlight, in the beauty of the Oriental garden, she did not care. She would revel in her solitude here, enjoy every minute as long as it lasted.

◆   ◆   ◆

She fed the animals, taking time to cosset the nervous cockatoo. The parrots were all growing used to her, even Mac. The African grey parrot watched her with what she almost imagined was friendly amusement. When they had all been fed, she coaxed the cockatoo onto her shoulder, enjoying the feel of the wiry claws gently digging into her shirt, the white feathers soft against her cheek. She set down some newspapers on the floors, then walked about the house with him. Angus trailed after her. At six, Claire cooked herself a spaghetti dinner, which she ate in the kitchen with Koko crooning and swaying on the back of her chair and Angus lying at her feet. Occasionally, she tossed a meatball to the dog, who eagerly snapped it out of the air. Then she washed up, finding pleasure even in little things like putting dishes back in their places and imagining where she would put things if Willowmere was truly hers. She rearranged a few things just for the fun of it. *I can always put them back before Myra returns,* she thought.

It was odd that she didn't mind being alone in this big barn of a place when being alone in her own home seemed so depressing. Claire turned on the TV for company but found she didn't need it and switched it off again. The animals made all the difference, she decided.

She returned Koko to the aviary, locked up the house, and turned all the lights out one by one. In the drawing room, she stood for a while, staring up at the portrait. It was impossible to tell if the small, extra details she thought she'd seen in the dream-vision were really there. The painting was too dark with age. Alice *was* wearing a necklace, but not the pearl pendant from the dream—this was a much fussier affair with several swags of pearls and dangling jewels. No, Claire hadn't had some kind of mystical vision, just a strange hallucination. How could she ever have believed it to be anything else? A rational explanation for everything, Dad had said.

And then, even as she thought this, it happened again. As she turned away from the painting, she felt a curious giddy sensation, as though something inside her head had slipped out of place. Her vision swam, the portrait became a coloured blur.

There was no time for amazement, surprise, or fear . . .

She stood gazing out across the sloping lawn, towards the stone gate and the heather-purple hills beyond. Then slowly she walked down the gravelled drive and out of the gate, pausing to look up at the stone lions standing watch there. Her grandfather had erected them as a sign that the Ramsays boasted MacGregor blood. But after the battle of Glenfruin two years ago, the MacGregor name had been outlawed in Scotland, and her family had scrambled to conceal its connection to the persecuted clan. Her father, however, had never forgotten his heritage, nor his boyhood dreams of taking the throne—though now he had to dream of his son or grandson becoming king, not himself.

The sound of laughter carried up the hill. Children were playing down in the village, swimming together in the sparkling waters of the burn. It must be nice, she thought wistfully, to have friends. As a little girl, she had longed to join in the village games. But she was a laird's daughter and could not have anything to do with the children of her father's tenants. She paused and looked back at the castellated towers of Glenlyon—another nod to her family's royal aspirations, like the crowned lions and the royal blue gowns that Father made her and her little half-sisters, Agnes and Margaret, wear. Even her name, Alice, meant "princess." In the old days, when the MacGregor clan still thrived, her nurse used to tell her that her father had the royal blood, which meant that Alice was truly a princess by rights. And now clan MacGregor was all destroyed or put to flight, so there would be no other claimants of that line. And the English no longer had a royal line of their own, so the Scottish king ruled both countries. It was no surprise that her father's forbidden ambition had grown. To see his heir rule all of Britain!

Though why a queen could not rule just as well as a king, Alice had often wondered. There was the late Queen Bess of England, after all, and her doomed rival, Mary Queen of Scots. Why did Father's ambition demand a male heir only? Well, it did not really matter. She had never shared his desire for the throne. Her own heart's desire was for one thing only: freedom. And that she could never have.

Her garments today were less confining than the elaborate dress she wore on formal occasions, but they were still far from comfortable; her black velvet bodice was stiff with whalebone, and her skirt, though not as large as the farthingale of her best gown, fell in long heavy folds from its wide waist pad. Her long hair was bound up under a cap of velvet lined with lace. She yearned to tear off the hot headgear and let her hair flow in the breeze. As she walked down the heather-clad hill, holding up her voluminous skirts, the white cat came running to meet her and rub against her ankles. She smiled. At least there was Leo—now that he had a body, he was more like a real friend and not some imaginary playmate she might have invented for herself. She bent to pet him, and the old, beloved voice of her dearest companion spoke within her mind:

"Alice, you have been a little careless, I think. You should not speak of me to others," *Leo chided.*

"I said very little, Leo. I so long to share you with someone! And Will is a dear friend. I trust him as I can trust no one else."

"He is right that some may see it as witchcraft. This is a dangerous age you live in, Alice."

"He will not betray us. And no other soul knows of you."

"I hope not. The consequences for you could be grave. Have a care!"

"I wish I could leave this place! Will is leaving soon," she said, smitten anew with sadness at the thought, *"for Virginia."* Ah, the New World! It was like the old fairy stories. Nurse, who was Irish, had told her of wondrous magical lands that lay where the sun set. Not that the real New World was anything like the nursery tales, but still it had an aura of romance. *"Oh, Leo, how I wish I could travel to the Colonies! Not merely to follow Will, much as I love him, but also to see the great virgin forests, the wilderness that no man has tamed."*

"I regret I cannot take you there. But I could show these things to you, if you like," *said Leo.*

"You could?" she asked eagerly, sitting down on a flat stone in the meadow and spreading her heavy skirts.

"I can place pictures of the great western continent in your mind. I can show you parts of it that even the explorers have not yet discovered."

"You have been there, Leo?"

"You forget: I do not go to places. I am neither here nor there, but in my own dimension. But I, and other beings of my realm, can touch the minds of living creatures on this plane and, through them, perceive the places they inhabit. And all these images I receive—both directly from beasts and birds, and also those images my fellow beings receive and pass on to me—I can in turn pass on to your mind."

Alice's breathing quickened with excitement and the longing to see, to know. "Show me," she implored.

"Close your eyes," *said Leo.*

She obeyed. Into her mind there came an image, like something glimpsed in a dream. A place full of tall trees and undergrowth. It was a scene at once familiar and alien, like and still not like the woods near her home. A bird shaped like a thrush but sporting a bright red breast flew past. On the floor of the forest a brown-skinned girl clad in loose clothes of animal hide was sitting all alone.

Leo's voice spoke in Alice's mind. "That is a young girl of a people called the Ojibwa. It is the custom for the young of her race to embark on dream quests, seeking spirit guides in animal forms. Usually it is the boys who do this, but this girl is special: she is in training to be a medicine woman, like her mother and her grandmother before her. Look, here comes the sign she has been waiting for, her animal guide."

A wildcat was gliding soft-footed through the bushes—a strange-looking cat with a short bobbed tail. It stopped and stared at the girl, yellow eyes intent, then slipped away again through the undergrowth. The girl straightened and stood up, an expression of transcendent joy on her face.

"How free she is, living there in the woods!" *Alice felt a sharp stab of envy as the image faded from her mind.* "And her clothing looks so light and so comfortable to wear. Ah, Leo, I am so glad you are my friend! I have longed so for a tutor, but no tutor could ever show me what you can."

"All the same, best not to speak to anyone of what you learn from me. The people of your country will kill anyone they believe is a witch—and her familiar, too."

"But, Leo, nothing can harm you! You are a spirit."

"I am, but this body I borrow when I visit your world is mortal flesh. As it is not mine, I cannot allow it to come to harm."

She stopped stroking the soft white fur. "Not yours?"

"I am merely a guest in it, as in a house. The cat that owns this body is my host. I look out through his eyes, as if through windows; I see all that he sees, hear all that he hears. Without him, I could know nothing of your mortal world."

Alice said nothing. A fearful thought had occurred to her. "Demons are able to possess animals and people, it's said. There is the biblical story of the swine that flung themselves off a cliff when demons went into them."

"I do not possess the cat. I said I am a guest only. I would do nothing to harm his body. It is a poor guest who does damage to the dwelling of his host! I can enter the body of any bird or beast. Only the human form is forbidden me. Hold out your hand." *She did so. There was a flutter of wings and a little bird, a wild wren, flew down and alighted on her hand. Alice gasped, and the white cat looked up with interest.* "Now I am in the wren, not the cat. Do you see?"

An image formed before her eyes: her own face grown huge as a giant's, looming before her. This other giant Alice had one hand held out too. She was in fact seeing her own face and form from another's eyes. Her angle of view changed, tilting downward, and she saw a soft feathered breast and tiny clawed feet gripping a huge finger. She was within the bird, seeing what it saw. Then the vision faded away as suddenly as it had come.

"That is what I see, Alice, from the bird's eyes. Now look, I will return to the cat." *The wren gave a sudden startled chirp and flew off her hand, whirring away across the meadows. The white cat came and sat down by her feet. The wild, predatory gleam was gone from its marigold eyes; they were filled once more with the calm intelligence she knew so well.*

"What are you, Leo?" Alice exclaimed, staring into those eyes. "If you are not a demon, then how can you do such things?"

"What am I?" *The cat curled his body around her ankles, gazing up into her face.* "Thought. Consciousness. Curiosity. I am all that you are, in fact, with one exception: I have no body of my own to inhabit but can only use the bodies of others—like this cat and the wren. Because I am bodiless, I cannot change or die. I am not truly of this world, this mortal plane of yours. There are many other planes of existence, and the one to which I belong is very different from this. It is a dimension composed of pure consciousness, of beings who are all mind."

She stared. "I cannot understand any of that. How could—"

"Hush, Alice! No more talking aloud. Look, we are no longer alone."

Alice looked up. Through the purple sea of heather a tall figure came wading, his curly hair dancing in the breeze. He was dressed peasant-style, in a belted plaid of soft brown that mantled his wide shoulders and hung to his knees. Will . . . It was William Macfarlane! She sprang up from her stone and hailed him as the white cat slipped quietly away through the tall grass. "Will! Will!"

He came up to her, but he was not smiling.

"What is it, Will?" she faltered.

"I am leaving for Virginia," he told her. "To manage my father's property there. I am ready to run it, he says."

Her heart turned to lead in that moment, but for his sake, she made her voice cheerful. "Ah, so the day has come at last, then. Are you not glad, Will?"

"I am not. How can I be?" His blue eyes were sombre. "I leave behind me what I love best in the world."

"I know how you love this place. But you will come to love your new home. Just think of it, Will—the New World!"

"True, I can love any land. That is not what I meant. I cannot live without you, Princess Alice."

Her heart, lead-heavy an instant ago, seemed to burst asunder. For an instant, pure joy flooded through her. And then in its place came pain, worse than any she had ever known. "Will, no. Don't say such things. You cannot know how it hurts me."

"You do not love me, then? There have been times when we were together, when I almost thought—"

"I love you, yes—more than I can say—but, Will, you know I'm to be married to your cousin. It is already arranged between our fathers."

"I know it."

"Why did you speak, then?" she almost screamed. "I wish you had never said a word!" It was too cruel. To go into her joyless marriage now, knowing this—that the man she loved had felt the same for her—it was too much. She could not bear it.

She whirled and ran away from him. But tears flooded her eyes and she stumbled, unable to see her way. Sun and fields together were a watery blur. Down on her knees in the long grass she went, and she lay there like a felled deer, sobs rising in her throat.

And then his strong hand caught hold of her arm, helping her up. Once she was on her feet, she tried again to run, but he did not release his hold on her arm. He swung her back around to face him, holding her against his chest. She did not fight but let herself lean against him, his wool plaid rough against her cheek while his free hand pressed upon the back of her head, warm and firm, the fingers gently stroking her now-loose hair again and again.

CHAPTER 14

"THERE'S NOTHING WRONG with you," the doctor insisted.

Claire could not persuade her otherwise. Like the school nurse, Dr. Ames agreed that two nights running with no sleep could cause Claire to have minor hallucinations.

"But it wasn't the cause," she argued. "I couldn't sleep *because* I was hallucinating!"

Dr. Ames shrugged. "As far as I can see, everything checks out. Your reflexes are fine. No neurological symptoms—no sign of any illness at all. Between these episodes, you say you feel normal: no blurred vision, no headaches or dizziness?" Claire shook her head. "Level with me, Claire, won't you? You haven't been doing any drugs, for instance, or anything else you shouldn't be into?"

"No, I haven't! But there are those dried flowers—"

Dr. Ames waved a dismissive hand at the jar standing on the table. "Potpourri. Completely harmless." She gave Claire a penetrating look. "You're not using them as some kind of excuse, are you? You're absolutely sure there isn't anything else you've used, or been exposed to, that could be doing this?"

Claire sighed. She couldn't blame the doctor, really. Look at Mimi and her crowd, all the stuff they had tried. "I'm positive. There's absolutely nothing else I can think of, unless it was one of the plants in the conservatory."

"Highly unlikely. You say you barely touched those. To be affected by a hallucinogen, you would have to consume part of a plant or smoke it like a cigarette."

Or rub it on, Claire thought, recalling the witches' ointment.

Dr. Ames began to write on a prescription pad. "I'm going to try you on a sleeping pill, see how you feel in a couple of days. If there's no improvement, I'm going to arrange for an EEG, just to make sure. But see what a good night's sleep does first." She tore off the page and handed it to Claire. "Let me know how it goes."

Claire left the doctor's office feeling dissatisfied. She was still certain that there was something in Myra's house that was doing something to her. She recalled yesterday's vivid vision, and a little quiver ran through her. All that morning, she had imagined that she still felt coarse wool against her cheek and the warmth of a man's hand stroking the back of her head. She could not get the sensations out of her mind, nor the reaction she felt whenever she recalled them. It was as if her whole body was charged with a restless, yearning energy.

◇   ◇   ◇

When she returned to Willowmere that afternoon, she felt a sudden misgiving. Angus met her at the door, not wagging his tail as usual but looking edgy and anxious. She made a quick check of all the ground-floor rooms, the dog following at her heels, but there was nothing amiss that she could see. No sign of a forced entry, no burglars hiding in any of the closets.

"What's wrong, boy?" she asked the dog. "Are you sick or something?" That was all she needed—to have to take the dog to the vet. Dad had left for his trip this morning, so he couldn't drive them. Once again she cursed her lack of a driver's licence. Angus whined shrilly and held out a neat white forepaw, looking up at her with imploring eyes. Then he lowered his head and began to sniff at the floor, pursuing some kind of scent trail.

She followed him into the kitchen, and there she saw that the heavy board she'd put in front of the cat door was lying flat on the floor. Nothing alarming about that: it must have just slipped and fallen. But as she gazed at it, Claire felt a little spurt of alarm. How long had the cat door been accessible—a few minutes or all day? Had any of the cats got out through the flap? Horrible visions of the great grey owl carrying one of Myra's cats off to its nest rose before her eyes.

"Plato, Aristotle!" she yelled, in a panic. "Socrates! Hildegard, Hypatia!"

They were nowhere to be seen, nor did they come at her call. Of course, they never did come when called, but . . . Claire shoved the board back in place, her heart thumping in her chest, then ran through the rooms again. To her relief, she spied Socrates curled up in a marmalade ball on one of the dining-room chairs. But there was no sign of any of the other cats.

She tore upstairs, the collie still at her heels. The tortoise-shell Hypatia was asleep on Myra's bed, and Aristotle, dignified as always in his black tuxedo, came sauntering out of the linen cupboard as she hurried along the hall. Good: only two left to account for.

Then she came to the tower room.

There were no cats to be seen in the study. But Al Ramsay's memoirs were lying on the floor, loose sheets scattered all over the place. Her heart gave another lurch. Had someone broken in, after all? The windows were shut; it couldn't have been the wind. Nonsense, she scolded herself. One of the cats must have jumped on the desk and knocked the papers over.

She went up the second flight of stairs to the third floor, with Angus following her. This floor was a huge attic divided into separate rooms, with high slanting ceilings and dusty windows and a set of steps leading up to a trap door—the entrance to the widow's walk, she assumed. She peered around crates and into old suitcases and boxes, anywhere a cat might curl up. Nothing. And the trap door was securely fastened. They weren't in the house, then: the cellar door had been firmly closed, so they couldn't have gone down there.

There was a sudden growl from the collie. Claire jumped. She had never heard Angus make such a blood-curdling sound, and she turned to him, concerned. "What is it, boy?" The dog was standing stiff-legged, with ears laid back and brown eyes glaring, facing an old battered bureau in one corner. Claire's scalp prickled all over. "There's nothing there, boy. Nobody's hiding under there. There's no room for anyone—"

The dog made a lunge at the bureau, and something squeaked under it. It was just an animal—a mouse, perhaps. As Claire ran to see, there was a pale blur of motion and a rat streaked out, desperately fleeing Angus. The collie leaped after it, snapping as the rat scuttled out of reach and down the stairs. Claire ran after them.

A dreadful squealing sound met her ears when she got to the bottom of the stairs. Angus had the rat in his mouth and was shaking it furiously. The frantic rodent was trying to fight back, nipping at the dog's muzzle. "Drop it, Angus!" Claire shouted. He ignored her, intent on his prey. She seized his collar and shook it. "Angus, drop it! *Drop it!*"

He let go, and the rat fell to the floor, where it lay motionless, apparently stunned. She scooped it up in her hands, being careful to hold it by the neck so it could not bite her: Angus's nose, she noticed, was scarred and bloody. But the rodent lay limp in her hands.

It was pure white, with blood red eyes, and rather plump. Not a wild rat, but a domestic one, the kind kept in laboratories or as pets. But Myra had no pet rats. Where in the world had this one come from?

She knew only one person who owned a pet rat like this. Was it Josie's rat, Herbie? Did that mean that Josie had been here, in Myra's house, snooping around?

She looked down at the rat, which was recovering from its shock and starting to squirm in her hand. Claire opened the door to the bathroom and put the rat inside, shutting the door hard. Angus stood outside the bathroom, sniffing and whining in frustration. "Good boy," she told him. "You stand guard." She went back downstairs, looked over the ground-floor rooms again, and then stood for a moment pondering. Nothing valuable was missing, as far as she could tell. No one could have broken in: the doors were locked still and all the windows intact, including the glass walls of the conservatory. Had Josie somehow made a copy of the house key?

I'm getting paranoid. Completely paranoid.

Why would anyone, even weird Josie, break into a house just to toss some old papers around and deposit a pet rat? The whole thing was ridiculous. Claire mounted the stairs again and went back into the study. Gathering up the papers, she studied them intently. As if anyone would be interested in the old man's memoirs. Anyone like Josie and Co., that is.

"The whole thing is perfectly logical," he had written on one sheet. "Indeed, traces of it are plain to be seen in all the world's folklore. In Australia, the Aborigines taught me that in the Dreamtime, long ago, spirits took the forms of animals and interacted with human beings. And the Bedouin told me the Jinni are beings lower than angels, who can appear in animal or human form. The same is written of witches' familiars, also believed to be spirits. And more examples can be found the world over. Mere cultural cross-pollination isn't an adequate explanation. Fairies, Jinni, familiars, daimons: all these are merely different words for a race of real immortal beings whom our species first encountered in its infancy." For the first time, Claire noticed that there were Post-it Notes on some of the pages. Myra was singling out some entries for special attention, it seemed. She picked another sheet up.

"I was much troubled in those early years by strange visions. They came to me when I was resting or at the edge of sleep, when mind and body were relaxed. They were not dreams. They were much too precise, too clear for that. And I had what seemed like strange delusions. At times, I thought Ben the parrot was gazing at me with a kind of intense, more-than-avian intelligence. African greys are very bright for birds, and yet I kept thinking of the African headman, of his talk about this bird being my *ukpong,* my bush soul.

Nonsense, of course, I said then. Imagination running away with me. Then I hit on an explanation: those herbal concoctions I innocently sampled over the years when I visited South America and Africa. They might have had a permanent effect on my mind, as some drugs are known to do. One or two that various shamans gave me were mildly hallucinogenic, like peyote. Now, of course, I have finally come to accept the truth and no longer attempt to rationalize it as the effects of some drug or other."

"A permanent effect." Could some substance or other have affected his mind all those years later? Claire felt a little stab of alarm. What if that was the explanation for what was happening to *her?* Myra might have innocently picked up the same exotic plants her uncle had tried years before — or ones that had a similar effect — and put them in the house somewhere. Claire really ought to go back to her doctor, and this time she would take Al Ramsay's writings along with her as evidence.

For the effect of the drug, or whatever it was, had to have worsened over time. How else to explain the next entry?

"The daimons are everywhere. I was warned that they would want to place me under surveillance: I know far too much. My own familiar does all he can to protect me, but even he cannot say which of the birds and animals in the grounds are possessed and which are not. Of late, I've even begun to worry about some of my pets. I'm troubled, too, about some crows that keep roosting in the big willow by the shore. They are so persistent, and nothing scares them off. They've taken to flying over the house, singly or in groups.

"Naturally, being telepathic, daimons can also create illusions. By influencing your mind and your subconscious, they can achieve nerve induction—alterations in the signals passing through your nerves. By doing this to the optic nerve, they can make you hallucinate objects that aren't there. By influencing other nerves, they can make you hear, smell, feel, and taste. But at least with regard to the visual hallucinations, I've discovered I have an edge. The daimons cannot quite compensate for my short-sightedness. If I quickly remove my glasses or peer over the lenses, I can see that the false image (being generated within my brain, rather than coming from the retina) remains clear and distinct, while the background recedes to the usual myopic blur. They've tried to correct for this, but there is still a brief lag, a fraction of a second, that gives them away."

Weird. Absolutely weird. Who would break into a house to read this stuff? Claire shook her head and replaced the last of the sheets. Then she went to the bathroom to check on the rat.

It was running around aimlessly on the linoleum floor, like some child's windup toy. But it limped as it went, its right hind leg apparently injured. What should she do with it? If it really was Josie's pet, she couldn't just release the thing into the outdoors. And it was hurt too. But she had no cage to keep a rat in, and she was not sure what to feed it. Besides, it should really be taken to a vet.

"Oh, blast!" she muttered.

Holding the writhing rodent with some difficulty in one hand and shoving aside the growling Angus with the other, she went back downstairs to the kitchen. There were some cardboard boxes by the back door, stacked for recycling. She could cut air holes in one, then tape the top so Herbie—if it *was* Herbie—couldn't escape. Then she'd call for a taxi to the animal shelter.

A sudden pain in her thumb made her jump and cry out. The rat had swivelled its head around and bitten her, so sharply that her hand flew open. The rodent dropped to the floor and instantly made a beeline for the outer door. She swore and ran after it, but she had lost precious seconds examining her bitten thumb. Even with its injured leg, the rodent easily got to the door before she could stop it. It nosed its way in behind the wooden board, which promptly slipped and fell flat again. The rat pushed through the swinging flap of the cat door and was gone.

Claire threw up her hands. It was good riddance, really. In the meantime, she had other worries. She cleaned the bite under the kitchen tap. Fortunately, it was not as deep as she had thought at first—just a nip on the skin between her thumb and forefinger. Then she replaced the board once more, this time propping a chair against it, and went out the front way to search for the two missing cats. Though the giant owl was nowhere to be seen, she could not get the image of her own injured, dying pet out of her mind. If one of Myra's beloved pets suffered the same fate as Whiskers, she would never, ever forgive herself, even if Myra did.

To her vast relief, she found both the escapees within about fifteen minutes. Plato was sunning himself on the paved edge of the carp pool, watching the fish with great interest; so absorbed was he in the show, in fact, that she was able to pounce on him from behind. Fortunately, he was a good-tempered feline and didn't object to being manhandled. Hildegard, however, was a different matter. She was playing tiger in the dense shrubbery at the east end of the property and absolutely refused to come out. Claire eventually managed to lure her into reach with an open can of tuna fish, then caught her by the collar and carried her off to the house.

There was, of course, no sign of the white rat. She had no intention of searching the vast property for him as well. If the owl got him, it was the fault of his owner, whoever that might be.

Once she had the second cat safe inside the front hall of the house, Claire closed the door on it and walked back out into the grounds. What if Josie was here, hiding somewhere? If that rat really had been her pet, Josie must have lost him while she was on the premises. It was possible he could have wandered here by himself from Nick van Buren's place, but somehow she doubted it. She recalled Nick's persistent surveillance of Willowmere and for the first time felt uneasy as well as annoyed. What were he and his creepy friends up to? What did they have against Myra? Did they resent her hospitality to the Wiccan coven?

She stopped suddenly by the front gate, her train of thought halted. The stone lions, their backs turned, gave her a strange prickle of déjà-vu. As she gazed at them, they were overlaid by a second image: another gate, taller and wider, but topped with those same rearing stone figures. Her breath came in short, sharp gasps; her head swam strangely.

Oh no, she thought. *Not again.*

She started to run back towards the house. But the house was not there. It had been replaced by the blurred ghost of another building, this one older, larger, with turrets and battlements like a castle. And great shadows, like the slopes of wooded hills, where no hill should be . . . She spun around, panting with fright. Castle, hills, gate—the scene whirled around her, wavering like a mirage, then grew more solid, more real. *Oh, please, not now! Not here . . .*

She sat on her horse in silence, staring out through the stone gates of Glenlyon and the blue hills beyond. How often had she gazed on the two stone lions as she headed out for a ride or a visit? And now she would not return, not ever— not if all went according to plan.

"We'll leave at night," Will had said to her that last evening as they stood together in the wood east of the estate. Over the weeks of their secret courtship, it had become a trysting place, where they could snatch moments together out of the sight of prying eyes, Alice's handmaid sitting alone some distance away with the horses. But the stolen moments were not enough, and so they had made their plans.

"A dark, moonless night, it must be," Will had whispered, holding her close, "so not a soul will see us go. I'll wait for you on my horse, outside your gate. We'll ride off together and find ourselves a chapel on the way. Once we're married in the sight of God, they'll not be able to do a thing about it. We can ride on at our leisure then, for even if they catch us, it will do them no good. And then—"

"To the sea," she murmured.

"Aye, the sea and the Colonies."

Every nerve in her thrilled at the words. The open sea and freedom, with the land of the west beyond and Will—her husband—at her side, with her forever. All their lives to be spent together in that wondrous foreign country . . .

"No," Alice said.

He loosened his grip and stepped back, staring down at her in disbelief. "No? You do not want to come away with me?"

"William Macfarlane, I'll go to the earth's end with you and farther! But you must not come here to meet me. If my father or his servants should spy you here at such an hour, or see me ride out to join you, they will guess what we are about. By night, it could not be taken for an innocent meeting. Will, you cannot chance it. You do not know my father. He can be so cruel!" She shuddered. "I will ride out by daylight so no one will suspect. They will think that my maid and I merely go to the village on an errand. Then I will slip away from her and ride like the wind to meet you on the road."

It took a great deal of persuading, but at last he had agreed.

"What is wrong, mistress?" her maid asked, interrupting Alice's reverie. "Are we not riding out, then?"

Alice gathered up the reins—and gathered her thoughts as well. She smiled at the girl. "Yes, yes, we are going." And Alice spurred her chestnut mare out of the gates, past the stone lions, which seemed to gaze after her in solemn farewell. Once out of the gates, she felt sadness give way to an excitement that was all the keener for being mixed with fear. Now the adventure truly began. When they arrived in the village, she had but to distract her hand-maid with some minor errand—a thing easily done—and then there was nothing to stop her and no turning back. Her old home would be lost to her forever, but it had never been a true home, and she would soon have left it in any case to be married to Alasdair. Alasdair! She wanted to laugh aloud for joy. She would be with William soon, would take ship with him and sail the sea to freedom with him.

She had brought the pearl necklace with her; it might be possible to sell it for money to buy herself other necessities. Her father might have bought it originally, but it was her mother's property and had been passed on to her, Alice, so it was hers by rights. It would be hard to part with the beautiful thing, her only memento of her mother, but then, her mother would have been glad to know her gift had aided her daughter, helping her escape to a new and better life than the one she herself had lived.

Leo had said he would come with her, but not in the white cat's body. He had left it, for he said the ocean journey would be too arduous for the little animal. He would be there on the voyage though, he promised—borrowing a seabird's or a dolphin's form, staying always close to her ship. Then, once in the New World, he would enter the body of an animal native to that land. He, like William, would always be with her.

As she rode, she heard a shrill bird call from the sky, and looking up, she saw a kestrel flying high above her, following her and her maid along the path. "Is that you, Leo?" she whispered.

"It is I."

She rejoiced that he was there, watching over her from the air like a guardian angel.

At the edge of the village, Alice pulled up her horse and sent the maid riding off to the apothecary's for a packet of comfits. As soon as the girl was out of sight, Alice turned her horse and headed in the opposite direction. Now she must make a break for it. But even as she prepared to spur her mare to a canter, she caught sight of some riders approaching. It was Alasdair's sister, Helen, riding on her brother's tall black gelding in her new brown habit, with her maid riding at her side. It was no use: Alice would have to wait for them both to pass. If they saw her ride off alone, they would surely tell her father—and she and William would be caught before they ever made it to the sea.

What happened next was so swift it would leave only a blurred impression on her memory for days to come. The grass at the roadside rustled and a fox ran out of it, moving so quickly that it was little more than a russet blur. It fled across the road, passing right before the front hoofs of Helen's horse. The black gelding reared up with a shrill neigh, sprang sideways, and then bolted away across the fields. The young woman screamed in terror but could not restrain her mount. Her maid only sat in her own saddle and wailed helplessly as her mistress was carried away.

Alice watched in horror, her own urgent situation forgotten. Helen was clinging to the reins and shrieking. She was too frightened to try to jump off, and by some miracle, she managed to stay in her sidesaddle. The horse laid its ears back, panicked further by its rider's screams, and tore off along the side of the valley at a hard gallop.

"She'll be killed, she'll be killed!" sobbed the maid.

Alice gripped the pommel of her own sidesaddle tightly between her knees and galloped after the gelding. He was far ahead by now, though, and her mare could not match his speed. People flocked through the fields, gawking farmers and shepherds, but all were on foot and none could help Helen.

Alice gasped, "Leo! Stop him!" Above her, the kestrel screamed and dived. For an instant she saw, in her mind, the hillside laid out before her as seen from the bird's eyes, with the two galloping horses and their riders far below. From that height, she could see clearly that Helen's gelding was now much too far ahead; her own mount could never close the distance. And there was a stone wall rising from the field beyond. If the gelding tried to leap it and fell, would Helen fall too and break her neck?

"Leo, go into him! Stop the horse!" If her friendly spirit could inhabit a cat or a bird, surely he could also control a bolting horse. "Please, you must help her!"

And then the horse halted. Right before the looming wall, he skidded to a halt, his hindquarters nearly buckling, his head jerking up at sharp angle as if an invisible hand caught and held him. Helen toppled from the saddle and fell, but the horse was standing still now, and the soft heather cushioned her fall.

Everyone gathered around as Alice rode up and leaped from her own saddle. "Helen! Oh, Helen, are you hurt?" The girl looked up, dazed, as Alice helped her to her feet. So concerned was she with Helen's safety that Alice was not at first aware of the grim silence spreading though the watching villagers. Then she heard the muttered remarks.

"Did you see? Did you see what happened? Like a miracle, it was."

"No miracle. Did we not hear her call on her demon? 'Leo, go into him,' she said. And the horse stopped, at her command! She's a witch—a witch!"

Helen gave a little cry and shrank away from Alice's arms. A big, burly man seized hold of the mare's halter before she could remount. And the crowd around her kept growing larger and larger, and again and again she heard the word "witch" come hissing from their mouths. Overhead, the kestrel was once more circling, uttering his piercing cries.

"Leo. Oh, Leo, what have I done?" she whispered.

CHAPTER 15

OKAY. NOW IT'S GETTING SCARY.

Claire stood outside Mrs. Robertson's office. The door was closed, but the light was on, so Claire knew she had to be there. She never forgot an appointment, so she must be busy with something. Claire glanced at her watch. Five after two. Well, she'd give her a few more minutes before knocking. Claire leaned against the wall and waited, feeling utterly exhausted. Had it not been for Dr. Ames's sleeping pill, she would not have been able to drag herself out to Willowville High at all. As it was, she had skipped all her morning classes and made another appointment with her doctor for the following week. She would show Dr. Ames the page from Mr. Ramsay's memoir notes and let her draw her own conclusions. She had also made this second appointment, to see Mrs. Robertson at two o'clock this afternoon. Not that the guidance counsellor could help: this problem was clearly outside her field of expertise. But

Claire badly needed to talk to an adult. She couldn't call her father—it would just worry him sick, and he'd be back in a few days anyway. But someone older, wiser, able to advise and give comfort . . .

The counsellor's door was still closed. Claire glanced at her watch again, frowning. It was now ten past two. Mrs. Robertson *never* kept her waiting this long. There was no sound of voices. She wasn't on the phone, then, or seeing another client. But the light was on—Claire could see its glow under the door. Maybe the counsellor had forgotten after all?

Claire knocked on the door. "Mrs. Robertson?"

"Come in," called a voice.

Claire stood motionless, her hand arrested in mid-knock. Then she flung the door open.

Mrs. Robertson was not there. Instead, Josie sat at her desk—in the counsellor's seat—idly painting her fingernails with black polish.

"What are *you* doing here?" demanded Claire, striding into the office. "Where's Mrs. Robertson?"

Josie glanced lazily at a shiny black nail. "Sorry, but your shrink had to leave. Family emergency. She left a note for you, there on the desk."

It was just like Josie to read a private note intended for someone else, but Claire did not waste any time telling the girl what she thought of her. She snatched the piece of paper off the desk and read it:

Claire:

I'm so sorry, but I'll have to reschedule our appointment. My mother's not well. I will see you as soon as I can when I return.

Pam Robertson

"Funny thing," remarked Josie laconically, "all these elderly relatives getting sick lately. Almost makes you wonder if there's something going around."

Claire looked at her with contempt. "What are you talking about?"

Josie got up, pocketing her nail polish. "You're running out of protectors, Claire. Soon you'll be all on your own."

With a final sneer, she swaggered out of the office. As she glared after the girl, Claire suddenly noticed that despite Josie's efforts to hide it, she was walking with a limp.

◆   ◆   ◆

There was no point in staying on at school. After the confrontation and her sharp disappointment, she was in no mood for classes. Claire walked across the street to the bus stop and stood in the shelter. It was growing chilly; there was a strong feeling of autumn now in the winds that blew from the north. But she was still so angry that she hardly felt the cold. When Mrs. Robertson got back, she would ask her to speak with Josie's parents. Claire had put up with a lot so far, but the girl had really crossed the line this time. She debated whether or not to mention the rat and decided against it. She had no proof the animal had been Josie's— nor was there evidence of any kind of break-in. The rat could have found its way in on its own, through the cat door.

As she waited there alone, two figures crossed the road and approached her. Josie and Nick van Buren. The former was still moving stiffly, as though her leg hurt her.

Claire glared as the pair came up to her. "Something wrong with the Batmobile?" she said, jerking her chin towards the black sports car in the school parking lot.

"We're not taking the bus," said Nick.

"Just thought we'd seize this opportunity to have a little talk with you," Josie began, leaning one arm against the bus shelter.

Furious, Claire swung away from them and headed back across the road to the school. It was bad enough that she might be suffering from some kind of mental illness or chemical contamination of her brain. She was not going to stand and be pestered by these two idiots while she waited for the bus. She would take a taxi. She had very little cash on her, but the driver could wait while she went inside for money.

But as she was looking through the public phone directory, she glanced out the glass doors and saw the black sports car drive out of the parking lot, with two figures in the front seat. Josie and her unpleasant boyfriend were leaving. Good. Claire closed the directory and headed back to the bus stop, where she stood shivering for another twenty minutes until the next bus arrived.

She was going back to Willowmere. Despite everything, she was still not quite ready to give up her precious solitude. It wasn't really dangerous. She would be just as alone in her own home, and for all she knew, Mrs. Hodge might be back the next day. She would have an early night and another sleeping pill, and next week she'd see Dr. Ames again with Mr. Ramsay's writings in hand. Maybe she could get a referral to someone who was knowledgeable about hallucinogenic plants.

She got off at the stop on Lakeside and walked, shoulders hunched against the cold, past the convent, the housing development, and the ugly grey mansion. As she passed the open gateway of the latter, she suddenly heard a voice call a greeting. She glanced up and saw a man standing in the driveway. Some hired men were raking leaves off the broad front lawn: he had evidently been supervising them, but he was now watching her. He was middle-aged and balding, with a grey goatee, and wore a very ordinary-looking cardigan and slacks.

"Hello," she replied, momentarily nonplussed. Was he just being friendly, or had he mistaken her for someone he knew?

He smiled at her reaction. "I thought I recognized you. You're my temporary neighbour, aren't you? Myra Moore's young friend?" He spoke with an accent that was hard to define, neither English nor German but somehow similar to both. Then she remembered that he and his nephew had come from South Africa.

"Yes," she replied, pausing at the foot of the driveway. "I'm house-sitting for her. I'm Claire Norton."

"How wonderful. I'm pleased to meet you. I am Klaus van Buren. Nicholas and I haven't needed any house-sitting yet—one of us is usually home when the other's away—but you never know. Do you think you might be interested?"

"Uh . . . I don't know," Claire temporized. She didn't much like the thought of staying in this house, but she could hardly say, "Sorry, but your house is too ugly, and I resent the fact that it was even built." Most likely, Mr. van Buren wasn't to be blamed for the look of the place. Lots of people wanted to live by the lakeshore, and there were only so many homes available. It was obvious, too, that Mr. van Buren and Nick did not talk much. He apparently had no idea his nephew knew and disliked her.

Claire's eyes slid sideways. There was no black sports car in the driveway, and the garage door was open, showing only one car inside: an elegant silver-grey model that looked as though it might be a Rolls. Josie and Nick were still out, then.

"You needn't worry; there is a very good security system in place," the old man went on. "It would just be a matter of making the house look lived in if we're both absent, keeping the lights on and so on. And feeding the dogs. You needn't decide right away, Miss Norton. Why don't you come in and have a look at the place? And perhaps have a cup of tea—it's rather bitter out today, isn't it?"

She hesitated. This might help. She could explain to this gentle, kindly man about Josie and his nephew ganging up on her. He might have a word with Nick, get him to leave her alone. If Nick's own uncle couldn't influence him, no one could.

"Okay," she acquiesced. "Thanks. I can't stay long, though, I have to feed Myra's pets and exercise the dog."

"Of course, of course. I won't keep you. Just a quick cup of tea and a chat."

"It must seem really cold to you, this weather," she remarked as she followed him towards the house. "Coming from Africa, that is."

He led her up the drive. "Ah, so you know about that! Yes, Nicholas and I made the move last year. We took temporary lodgings while this house was being built. We had visited this part of the world a few times, and thought we might like to settle here one day. Our own country is still suffering from considerable unrest, as you can imagine. But we were sorry to leave, all the same. Our family has lived in South Africa for generations. We're a bit of a mix—German, Boer, some English. But our roots in the country go back a very long way."

The house looked even more castle-like and forbidding up close. As they crossed the wet, leafy lawn, there was a sharp bark and the huge black dog ran around the side of the garage. It snarled at the sight of her, showing its yellowed fangs, but Mr. van Buren placed a restraining hand on its bristling hackles and smiled. "Easy, Rex. Don't worry, Miss Norton, he won't bite."

"He's . . . kind of big, isn't he?" Claire remarked, backing away a little.

"Yes, I bred these dogs for size and strength."

"You're a breeder? Then that explains it: I hear a lot of barking out back," she observed.

"That's right. I have my own private kennels here." He patted Rex's head. "This is a new breed I call a South African hunting dog. It combines German shepherd, Doberman, African lion hound, and wolf."

"Wolf?"

He laughed at her reaction. "There's nothing new about that. Wolves and dogs have been successfully interbred for decades: wolf-dogs are popular pets. Back home in South Africa, I sold a few of these fellows to the police for crowd control. They were, as you can imagine, highly effective. We also used them to guard our home compound. Security isn't such a worry here, but I still let my dogs out at night to patrol the grounds." He gave a thin smile. "Rex and his kennel-mates are, in fact, the security system I mentioned earlier. We need no burglar alarms. But I promise you that Rex will not harm you."

He stepped back, waving her in the front door. The dog followed them. Claire was uneasily aware of Rex's padding feet behind her. Despite Mr. van Buren's assurances, she didn't feel relieved at the news that the dog had been specially bred for ferocity.

The hall and sitting room were full of stuffed animal heads and skin rugs. There were heads of African antelopes, their horns rising in proud sweeps and gyres above their dull glass eyes. A lion's skin lay on the floor, snarling with open mouth, and a glass cabinet was filled with stuffed birds, monkeys, and other small animals. Mr. van Buren saw her looking at them. "I was an avid hunter in my younger days," he explained. "Nowadays, it seems there are only parks and preserves in Africa, and hunting permits are harder to obtain. You can't just go out into the wild for a day's shooting any more."

"I guess they're worried some animal species might become endangered," ventured Claire tactfully.

"Ah, yes. A bit too much hunting and poaching, and much too much development. A shame, really. Africa was once one vast wilderness, where one could hunt as one pleased. We have a way of ruining our own fun, haven't we?"

Claire didn't say that this was not her idea of fun. She sat quietly as he poured tea from an antique silver pot, chatting about the weather and other harmless topics, then she screwed up her courage to tackle the issue of Nick and Josie. She cleared her throat, feeling nervous. "About your nephew, Mr. van Buren. I don't mean to be rude or anything, but I wondered if you could talk to him for me."

"Indeed?" the old man asked, his affable demeanour unruffled. "What about?"

"Well, his girlfriend keeps bugging me. We go to the same school, and she just won't leave me alone. And lately she's been drawing him into her games, getting him to follow me around, that kind of thing. I wondered if you could please ask them both to stop."

The old man looked shocked. "I am sorry, Miss Norton. I wasn't aware that Nicholas was even dating anybody. He has lots of young friends, but no special ones I'm aware of."

"Her name's Josie . . . Josie Sloan. Look, I really don't want to make trouble for anyone, but she's being incredibly annoying, and it's gone way beyond just picking on me. I think she might even have broken into Myra's house. I found . . . something there that I think belongs to her. I don't know what her problem is, but if this keeps up, I'll have to get the school guidance counsellor and maybe the police involved, and there'll be a huge fuss. It'd be awful if she got your nephew in trouble too."

"I promise I'll look into it right away. Nicholas is a grown man and keeps a separate apartment in this house, but I know he respects my opinion. Thank you for alerting me to the situation. But do stay awhile and tell me about yourself. How did you come to meet Myra Moore? Did you attend one of her lectures?"

Claire explained about meeting Dr. Moore at the school seminar, and the old man nodded.

"Ah, I see. So your acquaintance is recent. You didn't know the old gentleman, then? Mr. Ramsay?" His gaze was keen, almost piercing, though that might merely have been the clear blue-grey colouring of his eyes.

"No, Myra's uncle died earlier this year. I never got a chance to meet him."

"A pity. You would have liked him, I think."

"You knew him?"

"Only very slightly. Like you, I came here too late to get to know him well. But I was most impressed by his wide knowledge on a variety of subjects."

Claire set her cup and saucer on the table and stood up. "Well, I guess I'd better be going. I have to let the dog out for his run."

He moved to a cabinet and opened a drawer. "Don't leave just yet. I've some things I'd like to show you: a collection of family treasures. Nick loves to show these to the young ladies who visit. A few are heirlooms; others I've picked up over the years, at estate sales and so on. I can never resist showing them off. If you'll indulge me . . ." He drew out some big velvet boxes and opened them up to show their glittering contents. There were brooches of various kinds, some with large stones set in them, and rings and bracelets and necklaces. Many were encrusted with diamonds. "My great-grandfather made his fortune in the South African diamond mines," Mr. van Buren explained. He picked up a ring. "This stone here might look to you like a sapphire, but it is actually a blue diamond, very rare. And the amber-coloured one on this brooch is what's called a brown diamond."

But Claire's eye had gone straight to something in another case: something that glinted and shimmered like moonlight and fire.

"You like that necklace?" he asked softly. "It's a beauty, isn't it? Seventeenth century, according to experts I've consulted. Would you like to hold it, perhaps?"

Claire just stared at the necklace in utter disbelief. There could be no mistaking that giant teardrop pearl and golden chain. It was Alice Ramsay's necklace, the one willed to her by her mother. Claire reached out and took it in an unsteady hand. Alice Ramsay's necklace, here, in her palm. She wanted to hold on to it forever, take it back to Willowmere where it belonged. Suddenly she realized the old man was watching her closely. How much of her reaction had shown in her face? Confusion roiled in her mind. She had to say something, fast.

"Holy *cow!*" she yelped. "I can't believe the size of this pearl! Is it real? It must be worth a fortune!"

He gave a slight frown. "I'd hoped you might be . . . impressed by its beauty. Young people are so mercenary these days."

"Seriously, though, have you had it valued?" asked Claire. At least this show of greed would explain her reluctance to give it back to him.

His manner turned abrupt. "I'm afraid not. Well, you must not keep Myra's pets waiting. Good day." He whisked the necklace from her hand and placed it back in the box, snapping the lid shut. "I will see you out now."

"Um . . . that's okay," she murmured as she headed for the door. "I can find my way."

She hastened down the passageway, afraid that he would insist on accompanying her. She felt dazed, punch-drunk. The necklace . . . How could it be *the* necklace? So far, she had been able to dismiss her "bad trips," or waking dreams, with logic and reason. But the pearl necklace—it changed everything. It defied all explanations but one. How the old man had come to get hold of it she had no idea, but that was unimportant. The pearl necklace really existed. It was not a dream, not a figment of her addled mind; the great pearl pendant she had seen lying on the velvet was the very same one she had seen when she hallucinated that she was the long-dead girl. It was real, and this meant that somehow, in some inexplicable way, she must have been given actual glimpses of the life of the real Alice Ramsay—had lived key moments of that life just as Alice had lived them, been invited to dwell within another person's skin in a time long past—

She turned sharply at a clicking sound behind her: the sound of claws striking tiles. The big black dog was following her, his malevolent amber eyes staring, staring.

A sudden blind panic seized hold of her. She made a dash for the heavy oak door and slammed it shut behind her.

◇   ◇   ◇

Claire almost ran all the way back to Willowmere. Her head was in a whirl. There had to be some sort of explanation. There had to be. She was losing her grip on reality.

This is crazy! It can't be true. There's always a logical explanation, Dad says. Always, for everything. That can't be the same necklace. It just reminds me of the one I hallucinated. How could I have seen parts of someone else's life? And all that about the magic familiar, Leo . . . How could that be true? It's all crazy!

But hadn't she asked for this, in a way? From the first moment she saw the portrait, she had longed to know more about the long-dead girl. And her wish had been granted. Was it some kind of ESP? Did the portrait and the old stone lions contain some sort of psychic vibration, echoing events from the dead woman's life? Claire had heard of such things—of people who claimed they could tell things about others just by touching their belongings. Or—she gave an involuntary shiver—was the house haunted, perhaps? Had the ghost of Alice Ramsay come to the New World along with these relics of her vanished Scottish home? And had her spirit somehow reached out across the centuries, to share the story of her life with Claire?

"No," she gasped through chattering teeth. "No . . . *no*."

She tore up the long, winding drive and, with some difficulty—her hands were shaking—unlocked the front door. She felt the familiar giddy sensation as she lurched into the hall. The pearl necklace, like the painting and the stone lions, had triggered a vision. She ran for the nearest chair in the drawing room and collapsed into it even as her eyes began to swim.

"No, please! Leave me alone . . ."

CHAPTER 16

THE TRIAL WOULD BE WORSE than the torture. For the latter,
they had not used thumbscrews or the rack but merely kept
her awake for three days and nights, until she was
exhausted and addled, bombarding her all the while with
questions. Only Leo had prevented her from signing the
written confession Morley set before her on the third day.
She had been too confused to realize what she was doing.
That had been bad enough, but it would be worse to face
the fear and accusation in the villagers' eyes, the disgust
and horror on the faces of Alasdair and his sister and their
parents. And no member of her family to give her support.
Had they meant to do so, they would have come to her by
now, given her some reassurance. Would not the glaring
absence of her own blood kin condemn her far more than
any spoken accusation?

Where was William? Did he think she had changed her
mind and decided not to join him? Or had news of her arrest

come to him? He could not also believe she was a witch, after declaring that he did not believe in such things. But if he came back to defend her name, what then? Might he, too, be accused? Once a witch hunt began, it was said, accusations flew like sparks from a wildfire.

Fire . . . she must not think of that. Not of the stake, the crackling flames all around her feet, the bitter, stifling smoke, the searing heat upon her flinching skin—

The door to her shed was flung wide, letting in a stream of cold, grey light and two cloaked figures. Alice sat up, feeling faint. She had been given no food for a day and a night.

"Well, witch," sneered Master King, "we have reached a decision as to your fate."

She stared at him, wordless.

"The evidence we have heard was clear, and every word of it enough to condemn you. The testimony of your handmaid was impressive indeed. The girl said that when you made her walk apart from you, she often spied on you and had seen you calling wild birds and other animals to you— she said that they came to you tame and biddable, as though under some strange enchantment. She said that you spoke often with an invisible spirit, indoors and out, whom you called by the name of Leo. Her fear was real and unfeigned as she said these things, and she swore on the Bible that it was all true. The villagers also heard you command your familiar to enter the body of Mistress Helen Macfarlane's horse. It is no use to plead that you meant to help her. To use the dark arts in any cause is wrong."

"But you are a fortunate woman," said Master Morley in his dry voice. "The court will not likely condemn you to death. By royal command, the stake is reserved for those who use magic to kill. Also, your father enjoys the favour of the king, and though it is plain he has little love for you, he will not allow his family name to be blackened by association with witchcraft. An arrangement has been made that may yet save your honour."

"I am to be set free?" she gasped in relief.

"No. It is our recommendation that you should be put to the water ordeal, so that your innocence may be established once and for all. That will prevent the need for a trial."

"You know how it is done," Anthony King said. "You will be cast into the river. And the water, being God's pure and holy element, will either acknowledge your innocence by receiving you into its depths or else reject you if you are truly a witch. For water cannot endure contact with anything evil, but will cast it forth into the air again. If you sink, you are innocent; if you float, you are guilty."

"Of course, your limbs must be bound," Morley added, "so that we can know you are not feigning innocence by holding yourself down in some way. Anthony, take her. The people will all be gathered now."

"Now?" she cried, starting up. "I must go now?"

She could not have fought them both, even had she not been in so weakened a state. And there was no chance of getting past them to the door. In a blur of fear, she felt the coarse ropes drawn tight around her wrists, then her ankles. Master King lifted her in his arms and carried her out of the shed and down the hill to where the burn flowed wide and grey beneath the overcast sky. A great crowd had gathered on the riverbank. And William was there! He stood at the water's edge, watching with a white, drawn face as she and her captors approached. For a moment, her heart leaped. Then, as he stepped forward to try to take her by force from

King's grasp, two other, larger men came up and pinioned his arms behind him.

"Will, no! They will kill you too!" she screamed. He continued to struggle, his features contorted with grief and rage. Silently, she called out for her guardian.

Leo spoke within her mind. "Alice, forgive me. I cannot help you now. I am not all-powerful—no bird or beast I could summon could prevail against so many. But I will be with you, I promise. Through this ordeal, and through all that may come after."

They were at the water's edge. The crowd pushed forward, expectant. Master King hefted her casually, as though she was no more than a sack of flour. Then he flung her into the burn. She heard William's anguished howl, had one last glimpse of his face as she hurtled through the air.

Then there was a shock of bitter, bone-deep cold as she hit the water, and a grey darkness into which she sank . . .

◆   ◆   ◆

Claire moaned and stirred. Angus was licking her face and whining. She was slumped in the chair, her head resting on one arm. With an effort she rose, shaking. She felt sick and weak, and the interior of the room seemed pale and unreal. She needed fresh air. Slowly, she walked out of the house and into the garden, followed by Angus. It was growing dark, and chilly too, but she scarcely noticed. Her head still reeled with what she had seen and felt in this last vision. She sank onto a stone bench and buried her face in her hands.

Did Alice really drown? Did it really end like that for her? And Will . . . what became of him? For he must have been real. If the pearl necklace was, then so was he. The clear blue eyes and gentle voice, the strong, firm hand whose caress she had known—all real. And yet that same hand whose living warmth she still seemed to feel was nothing but dust now. William Macfarlane was gone forever, gone beyond recall. Claire moaned softly to herself, rocking back and forth. After all these years, she had finally encountered someone she really loved, really wanted with all her heart. And he had been dead for centuries.

Tears welled up in her eyes. Angus nuzzled her knee and then lay down at her feet, but for once she paid no attention to him. She could not think of anything but the vision and its terrible end. If Alice truly had died that way, it was monstrous, unforgivable. Centuries might have passed, but the injustice of it still cut her to the quick. There was only the faint and fading hope that it might all prove to be a lie— that she had just been having meaningless hallucinations, and that the whole horrible tragedy merely sprang from her own mind . . .

Angus growled, very deep in his throat. Then he gave a sharp, challenging bark. Claire glanced up. Two figures were walking along the tumbled concrete and shingle of the beach Willowmere shared with the neighbouring estates. The figures came from the direction of the van Buren house; as she watched in disbelief, they walked off the beach and right onto Myra's lawn.

It was Josie, and Nick was with her.

This was too much. It was not to be borne—not now, not on top of everything else she'd endured today. Her precious sanctuary had been violated. She dashed her sleeve across her tear-wet cheeks and leaped to her feet.

"What are you doing here?" she demanded indignantly as they crossed the lawn and approached her. "This is private property!"

It was Josie who answered. "We've got some issues to settle with you." She came forward, her right foot still dragging slightly as she walked.

"Such as?"

"Your attitude. The way you talk about me and my circle at school. You're starting to annoy us, and that's not a good idea. And you're not just endangering yourself, but other people too. Like the housekeeper's aunt, and Mrs. Robertson's mom. And that guy who works with your dad—the one who thinks he's got some kind of flu? Convenient, isn't it? Got your daddy to leave town. Next thing, it might be your dad coming down with something. Or the Moore woman. We can do stuff to people, and it doesn't matter how far away they are."

Claire glared at her. "I don't believe it. It's not true," she said, but there was a hollow sound to her words.

Nick spoke. "Claire, you've got to stop involving others. They can't help you, and you'll just wind up hurting them. You're in this alone." He took a step forward, followed by Josie.

At once, Angus rumbled menacingly in his throat and started towards the intruders. But Nick made a quick hand gesture, and the dog immediately swung around, baring his teeth and snarling—at Claire.

"Angus!" she cried in horror.

The dog's flattened ears pricked up again, and puzzlement replaced the savage glare in his brown eyes as he looked up at her. Claire recoiled, staring, and Josie laughed. "See? What're you gonna do—call the cops? What could *they* do against us?"

The girl raised her hands, as if she was snatching something out of the air. Claire blinked, tried to make sense of what she saw. Flames were running through Josie's fingers—real tongues of blue-tinged flame, and they didn't seem to burn her or hurt her. "It's a trick," Claire croaked, retreating as the other girl advanced. It had to be a trick. It wasn't really fire. Or Josie had some kind of protective covering on her hands. Or . . .

"No trick. It's magic, *real* magic. I can use it. I have the talent. So what do you say about witchcraft now?" Josie seemed to puff up like a toad, swollen with pride and power. "Cat got your tongue? For once Miss Motormouth has nothing to say!" She laughed again. "Don't get on my bad side again, if you know what's good for you. I can do a lot worse than that." She held out her hands, and the fire suddenly shot from them in two long, hissing streamers, as if her hands were torches blowing in a strong wind. The flames snaked towards Claire, and she felt the heat of them on her skin.

Instinctively, she flung her hands up before her face and twisted to one side, stumbled against the bench, and fell to the grass. Her glasses fell off. Above her, the twin tongues of fire licked briefly across the sky, then wavered and retracted into Josie's hands again. The blurred figure of the girl seemed to tower over her for a moment. Then Josie clenched her fingers into fists, extinguishing the flickering flames, and she turned on her heel and limped off towards the beach. The dark indistinct shadow that was Nick remained, but he said nothing, and she could not make out the expression on his face. For a moment he stood silent, then he too turned and left her where she lay.

❖   ❖   ❖

Claire slammed the front door and slumped against it, trembling. *Not real, not real. It didn't happen. It wasn't real.* She locked and bolted the door, ignoring the pitiful whines of Angus, whom she had left on the outside. One hand gripped her glasses; she had not even stopped to put them on before fleeing to the house. With quivering hands, she put them on now and ran into the kitchen for the phone.

The woman at the reception desk at Dad's hotel said he was out. Claire did not leave a message but put down the receiver again, her hand still shaking. What now? She could hear Josie's mocking voice: "What're you gonna do—call the cops?"

There was a list of numbers by the phone, with the names of Myra's friends. She stared down at them. One name in particular stood out: Silverhawk. Of course—the Wiccan priestess. She was a witch herself; she might know what to do. With a trembling finger, she pushed the buttons of Silverhawk's number.

"Brodie residence," said a teenage boy's voice.

"Hello," she croaked, wondering if she had the right number. "Is . . . is Silverhawk there?"

There was a pause. "Just a second. . . . Mom! It's one of those witch people!" the boy called.

There was a pause, then: "Silverhawk here," said the woman's warm voice.

Claire stammered out her story between little gasps and sobs. The other woman listened without once interrupting. When Claire had finished, there was a brief silence on the other end of the phone.

"Hello?" Claire croaked. "Are you still there?"

Silverhawk paused before replying. "I'll be honest with you, Claire. I've been a Wiccan for twenty years, but I've never heard of anything like this. Are you alone? Can you go to a neighbour's for safety? In the meantime, I'll talk to some of the other witches and see if we can put some kind of spell of protection on Myra's property."

"Okay." Claire's voice quavered. In a moment, she was going to cry uncontrollably.

"Just go someplace safe, love. Understand? I'll come out there tomorrow and see what I can do. Okay?"

"No," Claire whispered. "No, you'd better not. They said . . . they said people will get hurt if I go to them for help."

"These folks are definitely on the left-hand path," the priestess replied. "They're heading for a fall. Don't worry, Claire, we'll come up with some sort of protection for Myra's place."

"No, wait," said Claire. "I just thought of something—" She hung up the receiver before Silverhawk could say anything more and ran for the tower room.

◆   ◆   ◆

She sat staring down at Al Ramsay's papers.

"The daimons cannot quite compensate for my short-sightedness. . . . They've tried to correct for this, but there is still a brief lag, a fraction of a second, that gives them away. . . ."

Illusion. It was some kind of illusion. She remembered the flames—how they had flared and roared past her; the heat of them, the hissing, roaring sound. And the shape of the long, licking tongues against the sky. But she should not have seen that—not with her glasses off. Fire and any other bright light should look like a luminous blur when she was not wearing her glasses, thickly haloed and distorted.

She swept on, going from one Post-it Note to the next. These selected pages read more like journal entries than a formal memoir. She read each one, then stopped short at a passage that set her heart racing even faster.

"She's come, she's come at last! Alice has been born again, into my time! I thank the powers that be that I lived to see it, for she deserves a new life, if anyone does. Arrested, tormented, put to the water ordeal—all without benefit of trial! 'Exonerated' by drowning! I am glad to learn that the witch hunters got their own punishment, at least. To assuage their own grief and guilt over Alice's death, her family and the villagers accused Morley and King of murder, and they were tried for that crime and executed. So in a way, Alice was the cause of their destruction, and through her death, she saved untold numbers of innocent lives. Who can say how many more people those two monsters would have tortured and killed had they not been stopped? As for the town of Lyndsay, by a quirk of fate, it was itself drowned centuries later, forever lost beneath the chill waters of a reservoir in a kind of poetic justice. I feel that poor Alice is amply revenged. But what, I wonder, will be the story of her new incarnation?"

"New incarnation," Claire whispered. She read on:

"My familiar tells me that she was born a few days ago, right here in Willowville! But what, after all, could be more appropriate? She has family here, so to speak—me and Myra. Though I suppose we can no longer call ourselves her *blood* relations now that she has taken on a new body, we can still be here for her, comfort and protect her when she comes to learn the truth. How I long to make her acquaintance once she's older! Of course, she won't remember anything of her earlier life at first, the daimons tell me—not for many years. Her own daimon familiar, Leo, who has once again inhabited the body of a cat, will watch over her and wait for her to mature before he reintroduces himself to her and reminds her of her identity. I won't interfere. But to see her—to know that Alice's spirit lives again on this earth! And then there's the mother—she must be warned of the danger her daughter will face. The girl will be a great shamaness in this age, far greater than she had any chance to be in seventeenth-century Scotland. So there will be many dark shamans who will wish her harm. For her own protection, the family must be warned."

The last entry read: "It has begun. I've just heard from my familiar that the girl's pet cat has been killed. Last night, an evil daimon in a dog's body got into her yard and mortally injured the cat—out of spite, and also as a warning to Leo. The poor child will be distraught: to her it was only a pet, of course, but still dear to her. Little does she know of her own danger. Will she be attacked next? Was Leo the sole target of their malice, or have the evil daimons and their human accomplices guessed the true identity of the young girl he's been watching? I dare not delay any longer. The reborn Alice is still too young to understand; she would only be frightened. But I've managed to meet with her mother on a couple of occasions, and the woman strikes me as very open-minded. If I can persuade her the threat is real, she in turn might persuade the father to move them all to a safe location. I will get in touch with her as soon as possible."

Claire stepped back from the book, shaking. The mother. Her pet cat. And the date on the entry was three years ago.

About the time when Mom . . . She caught up the journal pages again and combed through them, desperately looking for more.

But at that instant, all the lights in the house went out.

CHAPTER 17

CLAIRE REACHED FOR THE PHONE on the desk and held the receiver to her ear. Dead, of course. They'd taken care of that as well. What was she to do? Her thoughts whirled in all directions, like leaves in a gale. A shaman, old Mr. Ramsay had been a shaman. Was it he who had sent her mother away? Or had the enemy abducted her? And what of Myra? How much did the woman know? Claire recalled her startled reaction to the word "daimon." If only she could contact Myra— but it was too late now. Her breath made a soft, despairing sound in her throat, like a whimper. If only she had not gone to the van Buren house, if only she had not seen the necklace . . . Had she given herself away completely, despite her quick attempt to mask her reaction? But how could she have known that Nick's uncle was a shaman too? She'd thought the Dark Circle was just a bunch of kids, with Nick as their leader.

She peered out the window. The big owl had not returned to the willow tree, but there was a small one perched in one of the maples by the border between Myra's property and the van Burens'. It looked very like the one that had watched over her home from the maple tree.

Silverhawk was right. She had to get out of this place.

Claire felt her way along the hallway and down the stairs, clinging to the banister. Her backpack was lying in the hall near the door; she snatched it up and hauled it over her shoulders. Then she went into the dining room and peered through the side window. She could see no sign of movement in the darkened grounds. She had to make a break for it before it was too late, get to Lakeside Boulevard, and run for her life. It would be dark—she could see from here that the streetlights were out—but that might work in her favour. It would make her hard to see.

She opened the front door. Angus lay on the step; at the sight of her, he whined and gave a tentative wag of his tail. She let him in, then slipped out herself and slammed the door on him. Across the gardens she fled, keeping to the shadows of the trees. But as she ran, there was a soft hooting cry, and she looked up to see the small owl glide down from its perch, black against the sky. Their spy, alerting them to her escape? She broke into a sprint as the owl swooped low overhead, hooting again.

And then a dark shape burst out of the bushes ten metres away and loped across the lawn in front of her. The black dog. He stood on the drive, between her and the gate, legs splayed and eyes glittering savagely in the dim light. In the same instant, she heard a chorus of yelps and howls. She dared to turn, and saw more wolf-dogs coming up from the shore.

Her nerve broke, and she turned tail, fleeing back towards the house. There was still some distance between her and the main pack. If she put on a spurt of speed, she would make the front door before the other dogs got to her. But a quick glance over her shoulder showed Rex was gaining on her.

She twisted free of her backpack as she ran, and as the black daimon-dog closed in, she flung it at him with all her might. He snarled and dodged the missile—and kept on coming. But then something plunged down out of the sky—something blurred and grey—and flew into his face, making him yelp and cower back. Claire took the front steps in two bounds, ran inside, and slammed the door shut.

Once she'd secured the chain lock and bolt, she sagged to the floor.

The black dog. The daimon in him had seen her reaction to the necklace and not been deceived. Was he alone, or was his warlock-shaman master somewhere in the dark garden? A sound of claws padding along the hall made her leap up, but it was only Angus, coming to see what was wrong. The collie . . . she couldn't trust him. Nick might turn him against her, as he had done in the garden. She took him by his collar and led him into the kitchen. She would shut him in here, and then she'd be safe—

With a crash, the board in front of the cat door fell down, and Angus gave a shrill, excited bark. The flap opened, and there was a long, dark head thrusting in. Eyes and fangs flashed, and the wolf-dog snapped and howled in rage, trying to squeeze as much of its body through the small opening as possible.

The collie lunged at the intruder. In the same instant, Claire ran from the room, slamming the door shut behind her. The wolf-dogs could not get in. But their human masters—the warlock-shamans—would be here soon, and it would be an easy matter for them to break down a door or smash a window. She could not hope to defend this whole house, huge as it was, but had to find a place to make her stand. She groped her way back up the staircase and through the upper hall. Her left hand touched something cold and metallic on the wall—the strange elbowed blade of a Gurkha dagger hanging on display. She snatched it down and clutched its hilt in her right hand, feeling her way down the passage towards the attic stairs.

◇   ◇   ◇

Claire stood within the railings of the widow's walk, gazing out across the grounds to where the grey towered mansion lay. She felt like the captain on the bridge of an old-time sailing ship, confronting an enemy vessel. Behind her, the trap door was open: there was little point in shutting it. They could easily force their way through. But they could only come up the narrow wooden stair one at a time, and that gave her a slight advantage.

The small owl had returned to its tree, but she no longer feared it. It had flown at the dog, buying her precious seconds and probably saving her life. Not an enemy, then. It must have watched over her house as her protector. She recalled the flying vision, in which she'd been shown the Dark Circle's secret gathering—all through an owl's eyes. And then the giant grey owl had pursued the one through whose eyes she had looked, trying to kill it. She stared at the small dark shape in the tree. A friend, an ally. Could it be . . . ? She thought again of Whiskers—of how human he had seemed at times, how insightful. He had always sensed, somehow, when she was unhappy: he would jump onto her lap and comfort her. And he had always been there for her, from the day she was born—as if someone had sent him to her. Had there been another presence there all along, co-existing with the cat, guiding him, watching over her through his eyes? A presence that survived the deaths of all the animals it inhabited, returning again and again to enter new forms in a kind of symbiotic relationship?

"Is that you?" she whispered as she watched the owl. "If it really is you, then show me. Fly to the next tree."

And the owl flew—over and down—to perch in a neighbouring tree.

For an instant, the world seemed to shatter and fly apart. Then the fragments fell back and rearranged themselves. But it was no longer the same world. And she was not the same girl—not Claire, not really. Not any more.

The owl hooted twice, softly, in warning. Claire looked out over the grounds again. The wolf-dogs—she guessed there were about a dozen of them—were forming a sort of cordon around the house. After a moment, two black-clad figures emerged from their hiding places under the trees. She recognized Nick van Buren's tall figure and the shorter, balding form of his uncle. She stepped back from the railing. They were challenging her, but did they know who she truly was?

Then there was a creak behind her.

Turning, she saw Josie come up through the trap door and stand there behind her, smiling. The white rat clung to her shoulder, its pelt gleaming under the moon.

"That won't be any use," Josie said, pointing to the dagger in Claire's hand. "Not against me."

Claire let her hand fall back to her side. The dagger clattered onto the slates. "Actually, I don't need it," she replied.

"No?" Josie flung out her hand, and its palm filled with flame.

Claire pulled her glasses down, peering over the tops of the lenses. The flames in the girl's hand were clear and distinct, with no hazy aureoles about them.

"Well? Go ahead, throw it. Burn me," invited Claire, folding her arms.

"Watch yourself," hissed Josie. "You know I can. I'll do it."

"Go on, then. I'm waiting. Or were you planning to bore me to death?"

Josie's eyes narrowed. Once again the yellow streamers of fire erupted from her hands. It took a great effort of will, but Claire forced herself to stand motionless as the flames shot towards her face. Not real. Not real . . .

There was no heat this time, and no sound. The flames flowed and writhed around her, but they did not burn. Finally, they retreated.

"Nice illusion," Claire said. "You could take that act to Vegas."

Josie stood gaping. Below, the warlocks and the wolf-dogs waited in silence. The girl's hands dropped, the fire vanishing from them as though it had been blown out.

"It's not real—any of this—is it?" continued Claire. "I've been doing some reading. The old man . . . well, let's say he left a sort of trail, and I followed it. Between his writings and the things he marked in his books, I've figured it all out. Most of it you probably don't know yourself. How much have they told you, Josie?"

The girl stole a glance at her coven members in the gardens below. Claire went on: "As I said, I've put it all together, and I think I know now how it all works. They've been there all through history, haven't they? Daimons, spirits, familiars—whatever you want to call them. Some of these beings are friendly and mean us no harm. But when others get into our minds, they can do stuff to us—make us see things that aren't there, or even make people think they're ill if they're too elderly or stressed out to resist suggestions. It's become a sort of game for these beings: to try to take over our world by controlling our minds and bodies.

"So an evil spirit gets into an animal's mind, say, or the mind of a person who's too weak to detect it, and uses the host's body to spy—looking through the eyes, listening to what comes through the ears. And if you're linked with the spirit, you can also see and hear everything it sees or hears. It's fun, isn't it, Josie—learning other people's secrets? You just lend your little pet to someone to take home or you sneak it into their house, and then you get to watch and listen in. You can repeat bits of private conversations back to people so you can see the shock on their faces, or you can tell them what you've seen them do. And they'll never, ever know how you did it. But I know."

Josie cast another uncertain glance at her coven members. *Now,* Claire called silently.

The soft, downy wings were silent, the wings of a predator that hunted by stealth. There was a piercing squeal, followed by an echoing scream from Josie as the small barred owl swooped down and seized the white rat from her shoulder. As the two girls stood watching, the owl flapped over to the top of the turret, the rat dangling from its claws. Josie shrieked again and turned deathly pale.

"One other interesting thing I've figured out," added Claire, "is that if you link with one of these spirits—join your minds together—you'll suffer whatever its animal host suffers. Something called nerve induction. Did you know about that?"

She had no need to ask. The girl had sunk to her knees and was clutching herself and moaning as though wracked with pain. Claire heard the murmur of confusion from the warlocks in the garden below.

"Don't worry, he won't kill the rat," Claire assured her. "I'd break the link, though, if I were you—just to be on the safe side."

"I d-d-don't know how," stammered Josie, cowering. "They do it for me."

"Go away, Josie. And leave me and my friends alone from now on."

The owl swooped down again on its soundless wings, and the white rat dropped, squealing in terror, onto the widow's walk. With a whimpering sob, Josie made a grab for it. There was a sudden warm weight on Claire's shoulder, and she felt a softness of feathers nestled against the side of her face and curved claws that gently gripped her sweater like the cockatoo's. Josie's eyes widened, and she tried to crawl away, clutching the rat in one hand.

Claire looked sideways and saw the barred wing, the big, fierce eye, and the hooked bill close to her own face. Filled with wonder, she reached up to stroke the owl. It leaned against her hand like a cat. "You see, Josie, there is no power—not the kind you believe in. Power's all in your mind," she went on. "I know, because I bothered to do the research. But you're just messing around with stuff you don't understand."

"It's not fair!" Josie wailed like a small, petulant child. "It's not fair! You can't have the talent. You're not a witch!"

"I prefer the term 'shamaness,'" Claire murmured.

Josie sprang to her feet with a bitter cry and ran for the trap door. In the garden below, the warlocks and their hounds milled in confusion, their circle broken. Claire stood watching them, alone there on the roof, feeling potent.

"Not alone," a voice said in her thoughts. *"You have never been truly alone."*

Claire sighed happily, caressing the owl's feathery neck. "Oh, Leo, it's so good to have you back again," she said.

EPILOGUE

Scotland, 1605 A.D.

SHE WAS SINKING DOWN into the dark. There was no fear now, no pain from chill water knifing into her lungs—only this slow and confused descent. Against the looming darkness images flashed. She saw the bolting horse go careering across the fields; she saw the stone lions at the gates of Glenlyon gaze after her in farewell as she rode past; she saw William's blue eyes looking into hers on the fateful evening when they had made their plans. Faster and faster the images flicked past, like the pages of a book when you run them through your fingers. The Hogmanay party last year, when she wore the purple velvet gown. Her first encounter with the white cat at the edge of the forest, and the mysterious joy the sight of him gave her. Father bringing home his new bride, and someone saying, "Look, there is your new mamma." Eating bread and milk out of her blue bowl in the nursery while Nurse sat in her chair by the fire. Her very first memory, of cradling a cloth doll in her arms.

The last image faded, but she knew now that she was not alone in this lightless void. Leo was there; she could feel his loving presence and was filled with relief in the midst of her sorrow.

"Oh, Leo, is it over? Have I died?"

"Yes," he answered simply. *"You have died. I sorrow that I could not save you. But I am with you as I have always been, and I always shall be. From your birth until your death, and after, and before."*

"Before . . ." The last trace of fear abated, leaving her filled with wonder.

"You have lived before, though you do not remember it. And you will live again," he told her. *"But in another body, in another time."*

"Will." For a moment, she knew pain again. "Shall I never see him again?"

"Perhaps—but it will be in a new form, in a different life. It will all be new and different the next time. But I will be there too—I promise."

Again she was silent, pondering this. There would be another chance. All hope was not lost.

She said, "If I live again, Leo, and have my choice of dwelling place, let me live in the land of the west!"

Nameless, bodiless, pared down to the pure essence of self, she floated free through the dark: a soul stripped of all the burdens of its former life, waiting to be born anew.

ALSO BY ALISON BAIRD

"Baird's writing is as elegant as C.S. Lewis's"
— The Hamilton Spectator

THE HIDDEN WORLD

Young Maeve is upset that she has to spend the summer in Newfoundland with her aunt, while her mom and dad try to work out their marriage problems. But when she finds her late grandmother's diary and a beautiful Celtic brooch that seems to have magic qualities, something strange begins to happen. Before long, Maeve finds herself in a strange land, Annwn, that her grandmother visited years before. There she discovers a world of legend where Celtic myths, tales of the sea and the secrets of Avalon come together in a fantastic and horrifying way.

0141302933

THE WOLVES OF WODEN

The prequel to *The Hidden World* features Maeve's grandmother, Jean MacDougall. It's 1940 and Europe is engulfed by war. Fifteen-year-old Jean is filled with the same anxiety that plagues the rest of the British colony of Newfoundland. On a visit to a remote village with her family, Jean wanders off and is magically transported to the mysterious realm of Annwn. Jean finds herself in the middle of an invasion by a tribe of Norsemen known as the Lochlannach. When she flees in terror, she finds herself back in Newfoundland. Whenever her anxieties about the war get the best of her, Jean finds herself back in the hidden world.

0141311800

PUFFIN
CANADA

Other titles of interest by

O.R. MELLING

THE SUMMER KING

Laurel Blackburn has come to her grandparents in Ireland to escape the sorrow of her twin sister's death. After a magical experience involving her sister, Laurel's grandfather tells her that Irish lore holds that Faerie is the land of the afterlife. Laurel is given a mission by a cluricaun, of the Clan Leprechaun, to find the last King of the West. If she succeeds, she is sure that she will find her sister.

0141304111

THE HUNTER'S MOON

Findabhair and her cousin Gwen challenge an ancient law and spend the night in a sacred fairy mound. But when Gwen awakens, she finds out that the Fairy King has abducted Findabhair. Armed with courage and her knowledge of Irish folklore, Gwen sets out on a dangerous quest to challenge the king and find her cousin.

0141309911

THE LIGHT-BEARER'S DAUGHTER

Dana is about to emigrate to Canada from Ireland with her father, despite her protests. If she leaves, how will she find her mother, who disappeared when she was three? As Dana grapples with her father's decision, she is unwittingly drawn into the world of Faerie. There, she is charged with an important mission. If she succeeds, her wish will come true.

014130992X